The Blue Planet Goes Dark

Zachary LeQuieu

ISBN: 979-8-89212-966-4

Dedication

Thank you,

To my best friend, Jason, my cousin Marcus, and my friend and boss, Curtis. Without your guys' help, this book would be nowhere near completed and probably would still have been sitting in my computer, waiting to be rewritten for the 50th time.

Acknowledgment

This book has been rewritten several times since I was in middle school. It was a lost cause and an idea with no real plans to go anywhere until 2022. I started rewriting it when I got bored of my games and wanted something to do again. After writing the first four chapters, I showed it to my friends and asked what they thought about it, and it grew from there.

Curtis, unknowingly, got me interested in finally finishing it and getting it published. Again, thank you for your help with everything, Curtis. As for Jason and Marcus, who spent long nights going over my chapters word by word, helping me phrase things better, thank you for your contributions. Lastly, I also want to say thank you to my editors, as they have been the best help that I could ever need. Going forward, I just want to let them know that I truly appreciate their help in making this dream come true.

Contents

Dedication....iii

Acknowledgment....iv

About the Author....vii

Preface....ix

Prologue....xi

Chapter 1: Hopeless....1

Chapter 2: No Armistice....16

Chapter 3: Madman....34

Chapter 4: Against All Odds....50

Chapter 5: The Savior....69

Chapter 6: The Mall....77

Chapter 7: The Bait for Dead....91

Chapter 8: The Rescue....102

Chapter 9: Massacre in the Barracks....110

Chapter 10: The Guilt....116

Chapter 11: Morgan....125

Chapter 12: Survival & Sacrifice....136

Chapter 13: One Kill Brings Two....146

Chapter 14: The Lab....158

Chapter 15: The Power Surge....171

Chapter 16: Evil Trapped 183
Chapter 17: Death & Ashes...194
Chapter 18: The Forest Rut.. 206
Chapter 19: The Revenge 221
Chapter 20: The Dead...235

About the Author

Zachary LeQuieu was born in Clarksville, TN. He is a devoted individual and tries to give his best in everything he does. During middle school, he moved a lot and lived in Kentucky and Kansas for some time. Then, he moved to Alabama to stay with his grandparents, where he still lives.

Zachary tried going to school two times. First, he wanted to study law enforcement. But because his asthma took a turn for the worse, he couldn't finish. Then he tried again, this time for cyber security. But the school closed, so he stopped trying altogether and quit.

Right now, Zachary works as an Assistant Manager at a bowling alley. In his free time, he writes books, having written his first when he was in middle school. He kept changing and fixing it over the years. But it never felt right until now. He is excited because his book is almost ready. He wants everyone in the world to read it.

Preface

The blue planet was a beautiful place, full of beautiful creatures. There were birds chirping their favorite sirens, watching as the life created for them slowly unfolded. Even the humans lived in harmony, maintaining peace with one another. However, some people were relentless, pursuing different mediums to accomplish various interventions and other discoveries. These people were always on the verge of discovering something new every single day. While many of them lived in harmony with every single organism that roamed around the planet, there were some that were bound to be catastrophic for both the environment and the people.

These catastrophes can disturb the very fabric of reality, changing and morphing into something very dangerous. But that does not keep man from always meddling with the natural flow of life. Such an outcome was promised when a team decided to create an elixir that could cure a multitude of ailments around the world. But little did they know, it was bound to create more obstacles.

Such was the dedication of Jason, an eloquent man whose case was to cure all the viruses in the world. He and his team were on the quest towards perfecting that vision, but unbeknownst to them, a mass genocide awaited.

Join in on the conquest that led to the collective demise of mankind, followed by the causalities it brought with it. As the world slowly de-morphed and decayed, the remaining survivors were forced to think about only one question that ran continuously in everyone's head: What would you do if the blue planet went dark?

Prologue

They say life is a mere fragment of a reality that's broken down into the past, present, and future. The three fundamental pathways of life that everyone goes through, from birth to death. Life is questionable, sometimes meaningless—and most times—rather simple. And so, we're made into humans. We are all a cluster of memories bonded into the blue planet. This planet conceals our secrets and keeps us safe. And so, imagine— What if the blue planet that we so dearly love goes dark?

"Jason! What are you thinking?" asked Dr. Zachary Taylor, uncertain of this man's thoughts though certain of his intentions.

"Oh, you know, same old bullshit about the future and the end and whatnot," Dr. Jason Foster replied.

"Come on, friend, we have a party to go to," Zachary said as he picked up his coat and proceeded to close up for the day.

"You know... I'll pass on this one. You go on, Zachary." Jason went back to his work, sighing once again.

There were obvious signs of stress, and Zachary was smart enough to put two and two together.

Zachary patted his friend's shoulder and asked, "What's the matter, Jason? You can talk to me; you know that. We've been friends for God knows how long."

Jason knew his friend's intentions were pure. Although, at that moment, Jason was genuinely alright. He simply wanted some alone time—time to think and to let go.

Zachary caught on quickly; the silence said it all.

"Alright, buddy, I'll leave you to it then."

He put on his coat and proceeded to walk the halls of Virus Be Gone. Passing by the massive portrait of the founder, Dr. Tony Hopkins, Zachary stopped to take a glance at the man in front. He couldn't help but relive the past when he once walked these halls for the first time.

There it was: Virus Be Gone, a company started five years ago by a scientist named Dr. Tony Hopkins. Devoted to fighting off viruses and finding the absolute cure, the company flourished under Jason's team. The 'A' team comprised Jason Foster and Zachary Taylor, both unique in their own skills and hungry to fix the world.

Still, hunger dies down after a while, and bodies decay to the bone. Nothing is fixed within the walls of this world, certainly not this lab. It doesn't take a mob to cause anarchy. Perhaps it just takes two to change it all, and that too in the blink of an eye.

Chapter 1: Hopeless

The team stacked up in Dr. Jason Foster's office. The office looked like it had been through a lot. The walls were covered in pictures of beaches, sunsets, and waterfalls. There was a rugged brown desk in the middle of the room and not a particularly interesting soul in sight.

There was a picture of Jason and his wife on the desk surrounded by four chairs, who had passed away last year from cancer. A computer was on one side of the desk, and on the other was a file cabinet.

Jason was a 33-year-old scientific research team leader who enjoyed running, poker, and writing. Physically, he was in pretty good shape. He was of average height with pale skin, brown hair, and green eyes. He was a resident workaholic; it was hard to separate him from his duties.

"Alright... we've got another case..."

Dr. Zachary Taylor sat down and took one of the files from the desk.

"What kind of virus this time?"

Zachary was a 32-year-old scientific research team member who enjoyed meditation, fiddling with Rubik's cubes, and baking. He was friendly and bright but could also be very stingy and a bit rude. Physically, he was in good shape. He was of average height with light skin, black hair, and grey eyes.

"It's not clear yet, but it looks like it might be a new strain of the flu."

"I think we should call the CDC and see if they have any information on this virus."

"That's a good idea," Jason said as he picked up his phone and dialed the CDC.

After a few rings, a woman answered, "CDC, how may I help you?"

"Yes, hi, my name is Dr. Jason Foster, and I work for Virus Be Gone. We are currently working on creating a cure for this new virus, and we were wondering if you had any information on it."

The woman on the other end of the line hesitated for a moment before replying, "I'm sorry, but we can't give out that information to just anyone."

Jason was about to say something but was interrupted by Dr. Taylor, "But we're the best in the world at finding cures for viruses. If anyone can help, it's us."

There was another pause before the woman responded, "Alright, I'll see what I can do. But I can't promise anything."

"While we wait, we should start looking into anything that could be related to the virus," Jason said.

The team spent the next few hours looking for any information on the virus, but they came up empty-handed. They were about to give up for the day when the phone rang. It was the CDC; they had some information on the virus.

The woman from before told them that the virus was first reported in Cuba a few weeks ago. The symptoms of the virus included a fever, headache, and muscle pain. In severe cases, there had been organ failure and death. They also had a few files about the virus and the current cases, but she did not have permission to release that information. But she would call again if she got permission.

"That's not much to go on," Jason said as he hung up the phone

"Well, it's something," Zachary replied. "It's a start."

"True, But Let us call it a night for now." Jason stood up from his chair and grabbed his lab coat from the coat rack. "We can start fresh in the morning."

"Good, I'm exhausted." Zachary slammed the file onto the desk and stood up from the chair, almost falling over. "See, I almost killed myself standing up."

Jason laughed as he walked past Zachary and out of the office into the lab. The lab looked like a disaster. Papers and books were scattered all over the floor, there was a large stain on the white lab coat that Zachary was wearing earlier, and a glass beaker had been knocked over. The lab was pretty big for its use. By the corner, there was a high-tech computer. In the middle of the lab were a couple of lab desks parallel to each other, with lab equipment like funnels and bottles, beakers, and microscopy slides. On the other side of the lab, they kept lab equipment like the centrifuge, Bunsen burners, and microscopes. They also had a small lounge with a TV and some couches for when they needed to take a break from working. There was a small hallway in another corner leading to the decontamination chamber.

"Looks like we're going to have to clean this up ourselves."

Zachary sighed. "Yeah, I guess so."

He followed Jason out of the office. Both of them started to clean up the lab before leaving for the night as they were exhausted from the day's work. They finished cleaning up and headed home, hoping to find some answers tomorrow.

The next day, the team was bright and early in the office. They had a lot of work to do, and they needed to make a cure for this virus before it spread any further. They spent the next few hours working but had no luck. They were still hoping that the CDC would call back.

"Hey Zachary, can you come in here for a second?"

Zachary walked into the office where Jason was working.

"Yes?"

Jason looked up from his computer screen. "Have you made any progress on your end?"

"No, I'm sorry. I've tried everything I can think of, but I just can't seem to find anything. Without proper files or the virus itself to test, it's near impossible."

"It's okay, Zachary; we'll find something. We just need to keep looking."

Zachary nodded, "Should we risk it like we did for our measles case a few years back?"

"What do you mean?"

"Use a patient and study the virus first hand, getting blood samples and such."

"Oh yeah, that was pretty stupid of us, wasn't it? We almost died last time we tried that."

"Yeah, but we have better protective gear and better technology now."

"That's a fair point. Alright, let me call Dr. Smith and see if he's willing to let us run our experiments."

Zachary went back to the lab and got back to work while Jason called- Dr. Smith. After a few minutes, Jason walks into the lab.

"Dr. Smith was going to allow us to see a patient for our experiments."

"That's great news!" Zachary replied. "When can we start?"

"As soon as possible."

"Will the patient be coming here, or will we have to go to Cuba?"

"The patient is coming here, but it will take some time for them to arrive."

"Okay, I'll get the lab ready."

Zachary and Jason spent the next few hours preparing the lab for their patient. They set up all their equipment and ensured that everything was sterile. They want to make sure that they did not catch the virus themselves.

A few hours later, their patient arrived. He was a middle-aged man who did not look very well. He was sweating, and his skin was a pale green color. He was obviously sick.

Jason and Zachary helped the man into the lab and onto one of the lab tables. They hooked him up to all of their machines and started taking blood samples. They were hoping that by studying the virus in his blood, they would be able to find a way to cure it.

The man was in a lot of pain, moaning and groaning in agony. The scientists did their best to make him comfortable, but they knew there was nothing they could do for him. He was going to die.

Everyone worked through the night, and they were finally able to find a way to cure the virus. They created a serum and injected it into the man. Within minutes, he was feeling better. The color returned to his skin, and he was no longer sweating.

They were exhausted, but they were relieved that they had been able to find a cure. They knew many people out there were sick, and they needed to find a way to get this serum to them as soon as possible.

They knew they had something special and needed to get it out to the public as soon as possible.

Jason walked up to the patient and started writing down data, "We will keep you here for a few days to make sure you're doing okay after the injections."

"Thank you so much. I feel a lot better already," the man replied.

"You're welcome, but we still need to be careful. This virus is very dangerous, and we don't want you to get sick again."

The man nodded, and Jason left the room. He knew there was still a lot of work to be done, but he was confident they would find a way to beat this virus.

After two days of observing the patient, the man had been much more active and talkative than when he first came in.

"Looks like we did it, Dr. Taylor," Jason said as he wrote down the last bit of data.

"Yes, we did it. We found a cure for the virus."

Zachary and Jason hugged each other in relief. They knew they had saved lives and would continue to save lives with their serum.

"One more night, and we can release our serum to the public," Zachary said.

"Yes, one more night and the world will be saved."

The next day, Zachary and Jason went to work with high hopes that this would be the day they could release the cure to the world, but as they came closer to the lab, they heard an unsettling noise, the sound of a flatlined patient.

Zachary and Jason looked at each other and then ran to the lab to check on the patient.

"No pulse," Zachary said as he got the paddles.

"We need to revive him; we're so close!" Jason replied.

"Clear!"

As the patient's body jolted from the electrical current, they realized something was wrong. The serum must have mutated the virus and failed. They had cured one man, but the virus was still out there and was more dangerous than ever.

"We were so damn close," Jason whispered as he looked at the patient's dead body, saddened that they had lost the patient and the cure hadn't worked.

"We will find a way to cure this; we have to," Zachary said as he walked out of the room sadly, having failed to save the patient.

They both knew they had to find a way to save the world from this virus, but they also knew it wouldn't be easy. They had failed once, but they couldn't give up. They had to find a way to beat this virus and save humanity.

"Get yourself to the decontamination chamber. I will go next. I am going to lock up and clean this lab," Jason said with a look of hopelessness.

"Be sure to send the samples of his blood to be analyzed. We need to find out what went wrong," Zachary replied as he started to walk away. He didn't feel like it was the right thing to say at the moment, but it needed to be done so they could ensure the cure was right.

Jason hit the emergency red button, forcing the lab to go on airtight lockdown. He knew it was only a matter of time before the virus broke out and killed them all. He could only hope that someone would find a way to save the world from this nightmare.

A slight noise from the office was barely noticeable, but Jason realized it was his phone.

"Jason's office," he said, picking up the phone as soon as he walked into the office.

"Jason, I need you to come to the decontamination chamber now. We have a situation," Zachary's voice came through the phone, sounding panicked.

"I'm on my way," Jason replied as he hung up the phone and ran to the decontamination chamber.

Once he arrived, he saw Zachary covered in blood and a man lying on the ground with a huge gash in his stomach.

"What happened?" Jason asked as he started to put on a hazmat suit.

"I don't know. I was getting ready to decontaminate, and then he just started attacking me," Zachary replied as he started to shake.

"It's okay; you're going to be fine," Jason said as he finished putting on the suit and went over to the man on the ground. He started to examine him and realized that he was still alive.

"We need to get him to a room. Now!" Jason said as he and Zachary lifted the man.

They got him into a room, and Jason started to work on him. He knew that this man was infected with the virus and that there was no cure. He could only hope to contain the virus and stop it from spreading any further.

A few hours later, Jason came out of the room and found Zachary waiting for him.

"How was he?" Zachary asked hopefully.

"He's dead," Jason replied, looking down at the ground.

"But you said that you could contain the virus," Zachary said with a look of disbelief on his face.

"I did, but it was too late. The virus had already mutated, and there was nothing I could do," Jason replied as he started to walk away.

"What were we going to do?" Zachary asked, following Jason.

"I don't know, but we have to find a way to stop this virus before it kills us all," Jason replied as he walked into his office and sat down at his desk.

The phone started to ring again.

"Jason's office," Jason said as he picked up the phone.

"Jason, what happened? Why the lockdown?" Dr. Smith asked frantically

"Dr. Smith, the patient turned and went crazy. He is dead now, and I believe that the virus has mutated," Jason replied, rubbing his temples.

"What do you mean the virus has mutated?" Dr. Smith asked, sounding confused.

"I mean that the virus is now more dangerous than ever, and we have no way to stop it," Jason replied as he leaned back in his chair.

"But what were we going to do?" Dr. Smith asked as he started to panic.

"I don't know, but we have to find a way to stop this virus before it kills us all," Jason replied as he hung up the phone and leaned his head back.

He knew that this was the end. Jason decided the best course of action was to call the CDC to clear the lockdown and update them on the mutation. He knew that there was nothing more he could do.

He made the call and waited for someone to answer. A woman's voice comes through the phone.

"This is the CDC. How may we help you?"

"Yes, this is Jason. I am calling to report a mutation of the virus," Jason replied.

"What do you mean by mutation?" the woman on the other end asked confusedly.

"I mean that the virus has changed and is now more dangerous than ever," Jason replied as he leaned back in his chair.

"We will send a team to investigate immediately," the woman on the other end said as she hung up the phone.

There was no way to stop the virus now. He could only hope that the CDC could find a way to contain it. The CDC swarmed the Virus Be Gone building an hour after the call, wearing Hazmat suits and detaining everyone in the building for their safety and that of the city.

"This is the CDC; we're here to help," said the woman's voice as it came over a loudspeaker.

"You have to help us; the virus has mutated and is now more dangerous than ever," Jason shouted into the loudspeaker.

"We will do everything we can," the woman on the other end said as the CDC team started to work.

Although the CDC worked tirelessly for weeks, they could not find a way to stop the virus. It had already spread to other parts of the city. Hospitals were overrun with patients, and there was no way to halt the spread. The government had ordered a mandatory evacuation of the city.

As Jason watched the city he had helped build being evacuated, he couldn't help but feel like this was his fault. He should have been able to stop the virus. He should have found a way to contain it, but he had failed, and now the city was being destroyed because of it.

He knew that there was nothing left for him here. He packed up his things and left the city he had once loved. He knew that he could never come back. This was his punishment for failing to save the city.

He would never forget the day the virus destroyed everything. He would never forget the people he couldn't save and never forgive himself for what happened. Zachary decided to join Jason, but he knew nowhere he went would be safe, and the virus would spread fast and wide.

"I just realized something," Zachary said as he touched Jason's shoulder.

"The patient had died. I tried to use the defibrillator on him, but it did not work. He was surely dead; how did he attack me later?"

"I don't know." Jason replied as he looked at the ground. "But, I think that we should leave this place."

"I agree." Zachary said as he started to pack up his things.

They left the city and never looked back.

Chapter 2: No Armistice

What comes after hope? After everything is said and done? The aftermath of what's left. What's left are corpses of decayed hearts and eternal suffering. Trapped into this loop of losing the ones you love and loving the ones you would eventually end up losing. Perhaps it all matters within the light of hope, whether it still shines or has now completely gone dark. Slowly, the world moves away from an armistice. Day by day, it decays to the core. There is no peace for the foreseeable future or, rather, a future that isn't foreseeable at all.

Time stayed still, yet days went by as Zachary and Jason watched the world around them collapse. Though the burden of fault was heavy, the two felt it on their shoulders. All of the destruction, the deaths, and the living dead were all their fault.

Zachary wondered what could have been done to change what had happened. Never bringing the virus to the United States? Never taking the case? Having a better location to host the patient? Questions and no certain answers left the two dwelling on their failure.

"Get up and do something, Jason."

Jason struggled daily with his presumptuous thoughts, though they weren't helpful in the situation the two were facing. They were trapped in this loop of thinking and rethinking their position and whether they were still worthy of saving humankind.

"It's too late," Jason exclaimed, sitting on the hilltop next to an old eastern cottonwood tree. He caressed the dark green grass ever so gently.

"Huh, it's soft," he thought.

In that nothingness, Jason Foster couldn't help but sulk in this peaceful feeling at a wrong moment in life. A moment defined by the decaying city in front of them. A city cluttered by the sound of screams, gunshots, sirens, and mourning of the dead. Cries echoed through the dark skies, bringing fear to the hearts of the surviving two.

Their thoughts continued to surround them, making them feel more guilty.

"What have we done?" Jason said in a low, disappointed tone.

Zachary slowly approached his friend, still standing yet gazing over the decaying city. He was shaking, and his voice was aching, yet he found it in himself to speak.

"We tried our best, Jason. We... tried our best. It's just, maybe, somewhere along the way, we didn't take the right course. Maybe we made a bad decision, or maybe we made a bad call... huh? But I think we tried, right? We tried!"

"Zachary! This is our fucking fault..." Jason got up and poked Zach from behind. His thoughts were now physical. Foster wasn't in denial. He could see everything clearly. He could see his fault, and he could see what he had to do differently. Yet, time was cruel, and it had set its course. Their futures were now intact. Choices were made—choices that had led them here.

"*Ugh*!" Foster punched the tree next to him. "Do you not understand?"

Zachary could almost shed a tear, yet anger was the now prominent emotion, and he spoke up.

"Of course, I do, Jason, but we need to focus on what's in front of us. Look at me!"

Zachary walked over to Jason and looked him in the eye.

"Now look at the city. Do you hear that? Those voices, those gunshots? *Damnation of a whole city is not on us*!" Zachary yelled. His anger was misplaced, though he was right. He was consoling a friend who was raging yet filled with regret.

Contrary to Zach, Foster wasn't always the outright voice of reason. He was more focused on the justification of clear outcomes. Though Zach's words made sense, Foster was trying his best to understand.

"I... I..." Jason looked to the ground, "I don't know if I can do this."

"Jason, look at me. This is not your fault. You need to be strong for those who look up to you."

"Zachary, what am I supposed to do? Just act like everything is okay."

"No, I want you to grieve. Mourn for the people that are dying and are dead. Just don't let it drag you down; let it lift you up. Yes, we are more than likely the cause, but this is where we are... this is who we are. We cannot go back. So instead of feeling sad for ourselves, let us go and *fix* our mistakes."

"There is no fixing this, Zachary..."

"Maybe, maybe not, but let's try..."

"Fine, but what do we even do now?"

"We need a plan."

The two sat under the tree and came up with a plan. They knew that they needed to find a way to get the virus under control and try to find a way to save as many people as possible. They also knew that this wasn't possible alone. They had to be together and come together as one. Zachary tried to work his mind, and Foster aided the cause.

"The first thing we need to do is see if anyone else has any ideas on how to fix this problem. Find like-minded people."

"And how do you think we'll find them?"

"I don't know yet, but the two of us caused this. It will take more than just us to fix it." Foster added.

"Alright then, what else... I'm thinking," Zachary continued, "Next, we need to look for a safe haven. To set up a base camp. With the supplies we have, it should be easy enough to find a place and get it fixed up the best we can before winter."

"Good idea, Zach, but it's a long road now. It's gonna take us time. And it's gonna take patience. Huh."

"Foster, until we're together, we'll always find a way."

After a slight chuckle, Foster began to wonder. "We've brought this on the world, and it's only right if we make sure to look for people and help as many of them out as possible."

"Okay, so we have a plan," Zachary said with a little bit of hope in his voice.

"Yes, we do," Jason replied, slightly more hopeful than before.

They shook each other's hand, gave a nod of assurance, and headed back downhill to start their journey to find help to make things right again.

The two knew they needed to stay calm and collected; the world was in complete chaos, and they were the only two people who could make a difference for now.

***

The world, as they knew it, trembled and shook. Criminals were using this as a free pass to murder and steal. The local military had a rough time keeping order, and the police were practically non-existent. Law had now become a thing of the past, and the present was what people fought for. Small pockets of people had managed to stay alive and fight back, but it was not enough. The virus was spreading like wildfire, and no one knew how to stop it.

***

Zachary and Jason walked through the city, careful of every noise and movement. As they got closer to the heart of the metropolis, they started seeing more dead bodies. It was a gruesome sight—body parts everywhere and blood staining the once-clean streets. They covered their mouths and noses with their shirts in an attempt to block out the smell.

The two continued onward until they reached what looked to be an old apartment complex. The windows were all boarded up, and a large metal gate had blocked the entrance. There didn't seem to be anyone around, so they decided to look closer. Zachary climbed the gate and looked down into the courtyard. It was empty, all the doors were open, and debris was everywhere.

"What do you think?" Zachary asked.

"I think it's our best bet," Jason responded.

They started checking all the rooms to make sure they were clear. Once they were sure of the surroundings, they brought in all their supplies and got everything set up.

"It's not much, but it's better than being out in the open," thought Foster.

This is where they were prepared to make their stand. This is where they would try their best to find a way to save the world. With all their knowledge and experience, they might just have a chance. Though chances were scarce, survival would be needed through it. Yet, survival was of the fittest, and it was a question of whether the two were fit to save humanity at all.

"Okay, we have a place to stay. Hopefully, it stays safe. It is at least a little protected. Next, we need lab equipment." Zachary hoped.

"Too bad we left our lab in the other city... and I will not return. You will have to kill me before I ever go back there," Foster said with a recognizable ache in his voice.

"We need to find another lab, then."

The two of them started going through the city, looking for a new lab. They knew it wouldn't be easy, but they had to try. They couldn't just give up— not now. They needed to find a way to fix this before it was too late.

As they walked through the city, they heard a noise in the distance. It sounded like someone screaming. They followed the noise, and it led them to an alleyway. As they got closer, they saw a group of people beating up another person. The person was begging for mercy, yet the group continued mercilessly.

Zachary ran into the alleyway and screamed at the group to stop. They didn't listen, and they kept going. He ran up and tried to pull them off, but there were too many of them. Trying to think on his feet, he looked around and saw a brick on the ground. He picked it up quickly and threw it as hard as he could at the group. It hit one of them in the head, and they fell to the ground.

The rest of the group turned their attention to Zachary and started to come after him. He ran out of the alleyway and back onto the street. He knew he couldn't lead them back to the apartment, so he just kept running. He heard them following him, but he kept running and didn't look back.

He ran for what seemed like forever until he finally lost them. Trying to catch a breath, he stopped and leaned against a wall. He looked back the way he had come and saw the group searching for him. In his heart, he knew he couldn't go back that way, so he started to head in the opposite direction.

He didn't know where he was going but knew he needed to find someplace safe where they could continue their work. He needed to find Jason and warn him about the group of people.

Zachary quietly started to move around, trying to find his way back to Jason, moving through an alleyway full of dead bodies. They seemed to be dead for about two days or more, but the summer heat had worsened the foul smell. The alleyway alone looked beat-up, dirty, and filled with graffiti. Luckily, the building looked long abandoned. The doors and windows were broken but boarded up.

"Do I go this way, or do I go that way?" he wondered. Just as he was about to pick a direction, he was caught by some people supposedly part of the gang.

"The boss wants to speak to you," one of the gang members said as he punched Zachary in the nose, knocking him unconscious.

Meanwhile, Jason went to the beaten-up man to check on him, but it was too late; the attack had been too much, and he was already in bad shape. Jason was trying to check the pulse without getting blood on himself, but it wasn't easy. Luckily, he was able to get to the spot without getting blood on him.

As expected, there was no pulse.

"Why did they do this?" Jason thought to himself. There was no need for this violence.

Foster then realized, "Zachary? Zachary! Where are you?"

Suddenly, people started to surround him. Most were using their fists, and a few used knives or knuckle brass.

"You are in the wrong neighborhood, pipsqueak," said one of them, walking up to Jason. "You and your friend will pay for throwing a brick at me."

"I don't kno—" he began to say, but the gang member slapped Jason across the face.

"Do not try to lie to me, pipsqueak," he said, pulling out a gun and pointing it at Jason's head. "Now, where is he?"

"I don't know what you are talking about."

The gang member got angry and cocked the gun.

"Last chance, old man," he said, lowering the gun to Jason's kneecap. "Where is your friend?"

Jason closed his eyes, expecting the worst, "I really don't—"

Bang

It was the sound of a gunshot. Jason went into shock, falling to the ground.

He then heard everyone screaming, "Run! Let's get out of here!"

"You will regret that!"

He did not understand what was going on but was too afraid to open his eyes.

"Sir, you okay?" a man said in his deep voice, standing over him.

Jason opened his eyes and immediately looked at his knee, not feeling any pain.

"It's okay. We killed him before he shot you," the man said as he helped Jason up from the ground.

Foster looked around, noticing the dead body next to him, then the man. He was of a muscular build, short, red-haired, and scary-looking. The uniform he was wearing indicated that he was probably in the military.

"My name is Sergeant Lynne. I am with the national guard. Looks like we took the right road at the right time, or you may have been in bad shape before we got to you."

Still in shock, Jason didn't say more than two words, "Thank you."

"So, what happened here?" Sergeant Lynne asked.

"I... I don't know." Jason responded, still shaken up from the event. "I was just trying to help this man who was being beaten up, and the next thing I know, people were surrounding me."

"Do you have any idea why they would be after you?" Sergeant Lynne asks.

"No, I don't," Jason responded, lying to him.

"Okay, well, we will take you back to our base, and you can tell us everything there," Sergeant Lynne said as he started to lead Jason away from the scene.

As they walked away, Sergeant Lynne asked, "By the way, what is your name?"

"Foster... Jason," he responded. "I'm a scientist."

"A scientist?" Sergeant Lynne said with a bit of surprise in his voice. "We could use a scientist at our base. We have been trying to find a way to fight the infection."

"Any progress?" Jason asked.

"No, every time we come close, the virus mutates."

"I will do my best, but I may not be helpful in this area," Jason said, feeling guilty and wanting to say more but knowing it would be a matter of life or death to say he was the cause of this virus.

Sergeant Lynne nodded and started to head back to base.

"Wait... my friend. Dr. Taylor."

"He is with us, don't worry," Sergeant Lynne said.

Jason sighed in relief and followed Sergeant Lynne back to the base. He was wondering what he could do to help find a cure for this virus, and he knew that time was running out for humanity.

The base was not a normal military base. It was more of a base of operations set up within the city, located in the Thomas S. Stoll Memorial Park. It was set up in such a way that it could be easily defended and had food and water to last them months. It was also a good location, close to the hospital and other places that would be important in their fight against the virus.

As they approached the base, Jason could see people working on setting up defenses and others gathering supplies. There was a sense of urgency in the air. He could also see injured people being taken care of by medical staff.

"This way," Sergeant Lynne said as he led Jason into the base.

As they entered, Jason was immediately taken to a tent where he was debriefed on what had happened since the outbreak. The tent was a 10x30 ft canopy with eight walls. The inside looked as if it was set up fast, with foldable chairs and tables and a board with some notes and pictures about the virus.

It had been three weeks since the original strain of the virus started in Cuba and a week since the mutation strain surfaced in the nearby city.

The virus had been spreading quickly, and they could not find a way to stop it. They had been trying to find people who may have immunity to the virus in hopes of finding a way to create a vaccine. So far, they had had no luck.

After being debriefed, Jason was told Zachary was still passed out from his injuries, but he was okay. It was not life-threatening, just that some goons had punched him.

Jason was informed he could see if Zachary was awake in about an hour.

He was then taken to the research tent about five tents down from the debriefing tent.

"I need you to look through all of our samples and see if you can find anything that could help us," Jason was told by one of the medical staff. "We are running out of time."

Jason nodded and started to look through the samples. He examined them for an hour before talking to anyone. He wanted to get some time to process what had happened, but there was none.

"There is nothing to report on any of these samples," Jason said as he walked away.

He proceeded to walk to the medical tent on the other side of the park, where they expected the worst to happen. He looked around, trying to find Dr. Taylor, but not seeing him there.

He went to the command tent back where he had started.

"Hey, Sergeant Lynne, where is Dr. Taylor? I did not see him in the medical tent."

"Oh, that is because he is not there. He was last laying down in the housing tents, down at the end of the park," Sergeant Lynne said as he pointed in the direction of the tents.

Jason reached the housing tents, which were just regular camping tents set up in a line.

"This won't end badly," he said out loud.

Just then, he heard panicked screaming coming from a nearby tent. It sounded like it was Dr. Taylor.

"Zachary! I'm coming!" Jason started to run towards the tent. He unzipped the tent and poked his head in.

Dr. Taylor, not realizing it was Jason, punched the intruder.

"That's for punching me!"

"What the hell, Zachary!"

"Jason? I'm sorry! I thought you were one of the goons that knocked me out. How did you find me, and how did I get here?"

"I didn't. The military did."

"Oh, well, am I glad that both of us are safe! I was worried."

"Me too, Zachary. I would have died if Sergeant Lynne hadn't come at the exact moment he did."

After explaining what had happened, they decided to get some rest. They were both exhausted and needed to clear their heads before figuring out a plan.

They crawled into their tents and went to sleep.

A few hours later, Jason awoke to the sound of gunfire. He immediately grabbed his gun and ran outside to see what was happening.

"What's going on?" he shouted at Sergeant Lynne, who was running towards him.

"We are under attack! The infected have found us!" Sergeant Lynne replied.

Jason could see the infected now. They were everywhere. People were running and screaming, trying to get away from the creatures. The military was doing its best to fight them off, but there were too many of them.

"We need to find a way out of here!" Jason yelled over the noise.

Sergeant Lynne nodded and led the way toward the back of the park, where a gate opened into the street. But when they got there, they saw that the infected had already surrounded it. There was no way out.

Jason looked around, trying to find an exit. But there was none. They were trapped.

"What are we going to do?" Sergeant Lynne asked, panic in his voice.

But Jason didn't know what they could do. They would all die here if they didn't find a way out soon.

He looked around one last time, hopelessness filling him. And then he saw it. A pickup truck stood abandoned in the middle of the street. The driver's window seemed to be bashed in, and the door was wide open. Maybe they could use it to escape if only they could get to it.

"Come on!" he shouted to Sergeant Lynne, running towards the truck.

The infected were close behind them, but they reached the truck and climbed inside.

Jason tried to start the engine, but it stuttered and failed. He tried again but to no avail. The infected were encroaching, and the team began to panic.

"They're getting closer!" Zachary warned.

"I'm trying, but it's not working!" Jason responded.

"It'd better start soon, or we are all fucked!" Sergeant Lynne panicked, fearing they would soon join the horde.

"I know! I know! I'm doing the best that I can here, so shut the fuck up!" he yelled at the team to calm everyone down but only managed to instill more fear among them.

Jason tried to start the engine for the final time, hoping for the best but fearing the worst. Thankfully, the pickup rumbled to life, and Jason changed gears and slammed on the gas, leaving the park and the infected behind them. They were safe for now, but he knew this was only the beginning. The war had just begun, and they needed to adapt to the world around them, or else humanity may be lost.

Chapter 3: Madman

The pickup truck roared down the street as Jason desperately tried to put as much distance between them and the infected as possible. He knew they couldn't outrun them forever, but he had to try.

"What the hell was that?" Sergeant Lynne shouted, still in shock from what they just witnessed.

"I don't know, but we need to find some place safe to hide, somewhere we can figure out what's going on and what we need to do," Jason replied, his mind racing.

"There is a military base not too far from here. Maybe we can go there," Sergeant Lynne suggested.

The military base was about two-and-a-half hours' drive from the park. It should have been considered a safe location if they protected themselves and had their guards up. Given that the base was far from any city, it should have had few or no infected.

"That's a good idea. Lead the way," Jason said. "Can we stop at our makeshift lab to grab our notes and supplies?"

"Okay, let's go," Sergeant Lynne replied.

On their way, the group passed by many abandoned cars and bodies. Some of the bodies had bite marks or gunshot wounds, but all were absolutely dead. It was a sobering sight, and it only made Jason more determined to find a cure for this virus.

When they finally reached the apartment, they found it still intact. It seemed that the infected had not been here yet.

"Thank god," Jason said, relief evident in his voice. "There's not much in here, so let's go grab our stuff, and we'll be right back; please don't leave us."

Zachary and Jason jumped over the gate cautiously, hoping not to run into any more infected or goons.

"Okay, now that we're alone, what happened, Zachary?"

"What do you mean?"

"Sergeant Lynne knew who you were when I mentioned we needed to find you. He said you were already with them, but you said you have no idea what happened or how you got to the base."

"Honestly, it was all a haze. After I got struck in the nose, I was in and out of it. It was a blur, really, but I think I had just enough time to tell the military guys enough to get to you, or at least a rough location of you, and they radioed someone else. I presume Sergeant Lynne, but I wasn't fully aware of what was happening. I could have been awake enough to mumble words but not remember them."

"Well, I'm glad you're safe. I'm not sure what I would have done if I lost my best friend." Jason said, pressing his shoulder.

"Me too."

They looked around the old apartment complex where they had set up, but it looked like most of their supplies had been stolen. The only things left were files and a few notes scattered across the empty room.

"Well, at least we get to keep what we came for," Zachary said disappointedly.

"Yeah."

They spent five minutes cleaning up the notes and then proceeded to pick up the files. They started to make their way to Lynne and the pickup truck, but as they were heading toward him, a car horn blared three times.

Something had gone terribly wrong.

"Lynne's in trouble. Let's go!" Zachary said as he started to run towards the truck.

Jason followed down the courtyard, seeing immediately why Sergeant Lynne was honking. A massive horde was approaching slowly, appearing to be hundreds, if not thousands, of infected.

"Shit! Let's get out of here before we get stuck," Zachary said, climbing over the gate.

"Guys, let's go! Hurry up!" Lynne yelled, waving to them to get into the truck.

As they got into the truck, they yelled in unison, "Let's get the FUCK out of here!"

Sergeant Lynne slammed on the pedal and sped out of there. They took a moment to breathe before realizing that the gas light had popped on.

"Great, just great. Now, what do we do?" Lynne exasperated.

"Well, we can't go back to the city, that's for sure," Jason said. "Maybe we can find a gas station that hasn't been looted yet."

"I don't know if that's going to be possible," Zachary said doubtfully, "but it's worth a try."

So, they started driving down the road, looking for a gas station. They looked around for about ten minutes until they found a gas station near the exit they needed to take to get to the interstate.

They pulled the truck next to a gas pump and hopped out.

"So how do we do this? I don't have a card." Sergeant Lynne asked, closing his door.

"Not sure if that would work even if you did have a card." Jason pointed at the pump, "There is no power."

"Well, that makes things complicated," Sergeant Lynne said, running his hand through his hair.

"We'll just have to siphon the gas out of one of the cars," Jason suggested.

They found a length of tubing and started siphoning gas out of one of the cars. It took a while, but they eventually got enough to fill about a quarter of the truck's tank.

Now, they were on the road again. It was safe to say that they were having a good time, but their worries were about to catch up to them. The group had started to run low on food. They soon needed to find a place to stop and forage for supplies. But that was a problem for later. For now, they were just focused on getting to the safety of the base.

The quarter-tank of fuel took them about an hour from the gas station.

"Well, that's all she's got," Sergeant Lynne complained, getting out of the truck.

"What do we do now?" Jason also jumped out.

Zachary exited the truck and looked around but saw an empty road. "The only option now is to walk the rest of the way. I would have suggested we grab another car, but surprise, there are none here."

He looked back at the truck, then to Sergeant Lynne and Jason. "Guess we better get going, then."

They all nodded in agreement and started walking down the road, looking for any signs of life, but all they saw was emptiness. They were getting tired but pushed on. They knew that the military base was their only hope for safety; they had to make it there.

As night started to fall, they were getting desperate. They hadn't seen any signs of life in hours.

"It's getting late. We need to get to a safe place," Sergeant Lynne said, exhausted and sweaty.

"And where would that be? In the middle of the road?" Zachary questioned sarcastically.

"That was uncalled for," Jason told Zachary while giving him a 'what-the-hell-is-wrong-with-you' look.

"Sorry, I'm just tired and sweaty; I feel revolting."

"Me too, Zachary, but no need to be rude."

"It's okay, guys. I understand." Sergeant Lynne nodded. "Let's go a little further and hope we can find a tree to climb and stay up high."

"Climb a tree?" Zachary asked. "That seems a little dangerous; I toss and turn in my sleep."

"It's a little dangerous, but it's safer than sleeping on the ground where anything can get us. We're too tired to take turns keeping watch. It'll be our best bet to survive the night in a tree rather than on the ground," Sergeant Lynne stated.

The three of them found a tree and started to climb. It wasn't the easiest thing to do while being so tired, but they managed.

Sergeant Lynne climbed first, then Dr. Taylor, and finally Jason. They all nested in the tree and tried to get some sleep.

It wasn't long before they heard growling. They woke up instantly and looked down to see a pack of wild dogs barking and trying to jump up the tree.

"What do we do now?" Zachary whispered.

"Well, we can't go down, that's for sure. We need to find something to scare them off or kill them with," Sergeant replied, looking around.

He spotted a branch that was broken and about to fall off. "I've got an idea," he whispered.

He took the branch and started hitting it on the tree trunk, making as much noise as possible.

The dogs started to bark and howl even more, then started to back away and eventually run off.

"That was close," Zachary said, letting out a breath he didn't know he was holding.

"Too close," Jason replied, almost shaking.

The three of them stayed in the tree until morning, when they felt it safe to come down. They were stiff and sore from sleeping in the tree but were alive.

"Well, looks like we have to walk again," Sergeant stretched.

"At least we're alive to walk," Zachary implied sarcastically.

They started walking again, this time with a new determination. They knew they could make it to the military base. They had to because their survival depended on it.

With the team walking, it was now a two-day hike from the park to the military base. Luckily, they had gotten over an hour before the car had run out of gas, so only half of the distance remained, but walking still took a lot of time.

They took breaks every few hours to rest and eat what they could find near them, but they eventually pushed on. They knew that time was against them.

Finally, they saw the base in the distance. They picked up pace, knowing that they were almost there. They were tired, hungry, and thirsty but didn't care.

As they got closer, they saw people moving around the base.

"They're alive! There are other people out there!" Foster thought.

They quickened their pace to a jog until they finally reached the gates of Fort Riley.

They were safe. They had made it.

"Stop, or we'll shoot!" one of the military guards shouted.

Everyone froze and immediately raised their hands.

"I am Sergeant Lynne, Bravo Company. We are from the temp site in Thomas S. Stoll Memorial Park. It was attacked a few days ago, but we were able to escape," Sergeant Lynne said, a little irritated.

"And who are these people with you?" the guard interrogated.

"This is Zachary and Jason. They're scientists," Sergeant Lynne replied. "They are looking for a cure to the virus."

The guard quickly reported the information to the base commander. They heard some mumbling; then the guard looked at them for a moment until he finally opened the gates and let them in.

"Welcome to Fort Riley," the guard said with a small smile.

The team was finally safe; they could rest and heal their wounds. They knew it wouldn't be long before they were needed again, but for now, they could relax and take a breather. Survival was key in these dark times. Who knew what the future held? But would be ready for it. Together, they would face whatever came next.

"Go to the briefing room. The commander is waiting for you," the guard said as he pointed to a building.

The team nodded and started walking toward the building. They had a lot to discuss with the commander a lot of information that could help save lives.

The building looked fairly old but has had some new work done to it. When they entered, they saw that the building had a main lobby that looked empty and a back room, the briefing room. The door was slightly ajar, so they knew someone was in there. They walked over and knocked on the door.

"Come in," a gruff voice said from inside the room.

They saw a man in his mid-50s sitting at a desk as they walked in. He had greying hair and looked like he had seen better days.

"Take a seat," the man said, gesturing to the chairs in front of his desk.

The team did as they were told.

"I am Major Jameson. I am the commander of this base," the man introduced himself.

"I hear you have information for me?" he asked, getting straight to business.s

Sergeant Lynne started to fill the commander in on everything that had happened, from the initial outbreak to their escape from the park. He told him about their research and what they had found so far.

The commander looked at them for a few minutes before speaking, "That is a lot of information. We will need to go over it in more detail, but I think you three have earned yourselves a rest. You can bunk down in the barracks and we will talk more in the morning," he said standing up from his desk.

The team stood up as well, taking a sigh of relief; they were tired and ready to get some sleep. They followed the commander out of the room and to the barracks. They were safe for now but knew the fight was far from over.

The next morning, the team was awoken by the sound of someone calling their names.

They saw a soldier standing at the foot of their bunk, "The commander wants to see you in his office. Now."

The team quickly got up and started to get dressed. They were still tired but knew they had to talk to the commander. They followed the soldier to the commander's office and knocked on the door.

"Come in," Major Jameson called from inside the room.

The team walked in and took a seat.

"I've looked over your information, and I think you three could be a valuable asset to this base," the commander started. "I would like to offer you a place on my team."

The team looked at each other and nodded, knowing they could make a difference and were ready to fight. They would do whatever it took to help save lives.

Major Jameson grinned. "Welcome to the team," he said as he shook their hands.

The team had a lot of work ahead of them, but they were ready for it. With teamwork and determination, they would prevail. The blue planet might have been dark at present, but they would fight for the survival of humanity. Together, they would make sure that the light never went out.

Sergeant Lynne was with the command doing some paperwork; Zachary and Jason were in a top-of-the-line research lab. The lab looked like it had been made for a hospital. It was all new and clean, with the best equipment that money could buy.

"This is very interesting," Jason said as he walked up to one of the lab tables.

"Yeah, I think so, too," Zachary replied. "Let's start by going over the data from the outbreak, and hopefully, we will find something."

They started reviewing the data and soon found something they had not seen before. There was a pattern in the way the virus was spreading. It was like it was being spread purposely.

"I think we should tell the commander about this," Jason said. "He needs to know what we found."

The two nodded in agreement and printed out the data, then headed to the commander's office. They knocked on the door and waited for him to respond.

"Come in," Major Jameson called from inside the room.

They walked in and took a seat.

"We found something we believed you needed to see," Zachary said as he handed the commander the collected data folder. The commander looked at it for a few minutes before speaking.

"This is concerning. I'll need to look into this further," he said, standing up from his desk.

They nodded and stood up as well.

"Thank you for bringing this to my attention," he said as he shook their hands.

Zachary and Jason returned to the lab. Sergeant Lynne was on patrol with some of the other soldiers near the main gate. They were keeping an eye out for anything suspicious. So far, things had been quiet, but they knew it wouldn't last. Suddenly, they heard a noise in the distance. They all got into position and waited for whatever was coming their way. Soon enough, they saw a group of people walking towards them. The soldiers got ready to fire, but Sergeant Lynne stopped them. He knew these people; they were survivors from a nearby town. He remembered seeing them before the outbreak started. He relayed this to the soldiers. As the survivors came closer, the soldiers saw they were tired and scared. They looked like they had been through a lot and needed help.

“We need to get them back to the base,” Sergeant Lynne told the other soldiers.

They nodded in agreement, and some started to escort the survivors back to the base. Major Jameson had seen the group of survivors coming in, and he knew they would need help. He ordered some soldiers to take them to the infirmary and set them up with a place to stay.

“We will set them up with jobs in the morning for those who can work,” Major Jameson said as he walked away and headed to his office.

***

Zachary and Jason discussed how this might be a bio attack, casting doubt and suspicion on every shred of evidence they had uncovered. Each day, they sifted through the data, searching for hidden patterns and clues that would unmask the culprit behind this insidious outbreak.

As Jason and Zachary pored over the information, a chilling realization crept over them. This was no accident. This was the work of a madman, a deranged individual with a twisted agenda and a diabolical plan.

“We cannot let this go unpunished,” Jason declared, his voice ringing with steely determination. “Whoever is responsible must be brought to justice before they can cause any more harm.”

Zachary nodded, his eyes flashing with a fierce intensity.

"We will leave no stone unturned," he vowed. "Together, we will track down this perpetrator and put an end to their reign of terror."

As they delved deeper into the data, following each lead with dogged persistence, a sense of urgency seized them. Lives were at stake, and time was running out. But they refused to be deterred. With their minds set on their goal and hearts filled with a burning sense of justice, they marched forward, ready to face whatever challenges lay ahead.

Chapter 4: Against All Odds

The team was gathered in the briefing room, tense with anticipation as they listened to Jason describe their dire situation. The zombie apocalypse had spread worldwide, and it was only a matter of time before it reached their base. The team knew they needed to find a way to stop the virus before it was too late.

"We need to find a cure and figure out who or what started this," Jason declared, his voice tight with urgency.

"But how?" Sergeant Lynne asked, his brow furrowed in concern.

"I don't know," Jason admitted, "but we have to try. We must find a way to stop this virus from spreading further."

As the team huddled together, Zachary and Jason couldn't help but feel a sense of guilt and regret. They knew their mistake had been used as a deadly bioweapon, and they couldn't shake the feeling that they were somehow responsible for the disaster that had befallen the world.

"How did this happen?" Zachary whispered to himself, his heart heavy with sorrow.

"I think it's time we told you our secret," Jason announced suddenly, drawing the attention of everyone in the briefing room.

The major, Sergeant Lynne, a few soldiers standing guard, and, of course, Zachary all turned to look at him.

"You sure, Jason? This may not end well for us," Zachary whispered urgently into Jason's ear.

"Yeah," Jason said firmly, his voice unwavering.

"We work for Virus Be Gone."

As Jason continued to explain their involvement with the virus, the major's eyes widened with recognition. He already knew something about their work, and the revelation only confirmed his suspicions.

"We were working on a cure," Jason explained, his tone earnest.

"While we waited for the CDC to transfer us some files we needed, we decided we could try to study the virus first-hand. We brought a man infected with the original strain from Cuba to our lab. We took the necessary precautions to contain the virus, or at least, that is what we thought. We made a cure that worked for two-and-a-half days. When we were getting ready to release it in the morning, something went wrong, and the patient died, then later tried to attack us. Our city was the first to get hit with the newly mutated virus."

The room fell silent as Jason finished speaking. Major Jameson was the first to break the stillness.

"Well, that is something," he said, his voice heavy with sarcasm.

Zachary looked worried, knowing that something terrible was about to happen to them. He wanted to joke about not making things worse but knew it wouldn't be the right time.

"It won't be long before the infected get to this base," Major Jameson said seriously.

"Use our research lab and ask any of the lab techs or soldiers to get what you need to make another cure. We need it as soon as possible."

As Sergeant Lynne left for patrol, the doctors returned to the research lab to continue their work. But despite their best efforts, they could not progress in finding a cure.

"We're running out of time," Jason said, his voice strained with exhaustion.

"I know," Zachary replied, "but we can't give up. We have to keep trying."

Desperate to find a solution, Zachary headed towards the operation room, where he could hear an argument brewing between Sergeant Lynne and Major Jameson. As he approached, he could sense the tension in the air.

"Your platoon is dead. You are no longer a sergeant," Major Jameson said violently, grabbing a folder and throwing it across the room.

"You left your platoon at the park to save some scientists, abandoning your duty."

Sergeant Lynne grabbed his bag and stormed out, saying, "I'll prove you all wrong. My team met an early grave due to a virus your team caused. You better hope those scientists never find out you caused it. They may not help you fix your mistake trying to make a weapon."

"You have no proof; they have no proof. Dr. Smith was the one with his hands dirty. He injected the patient who was cured of the virus with something that mutated it, making it more deadly and killing the man. He told me everyone from Virus Be Gone was dead," Major Jameson said, "but that didn't matter then!"

"You knew it was your fault," Sergeant Lynne informed as he left the room, noticing Zachary trying to hide but saying nothing and kept walking.

Major Jameson rolled his eyes and turned to the barely functional computer.

"Low on power and resources," he said, "and only two days were projected for the infected to reach this base."

Zachary went back into the lab a few moments later. "I... have some bad news," he told Jason.

"What was it?" Jason asked.

"The base is going to be attacked in two days," Zachary said. "We needed to find a cure before then; however, we are no closer to finding a cure now than we were when we started."

"I know, and it has gotten worse," Zachary said, "Major Jameson's team was the one that made the virus; they were making a weapon."

"So, it is their fault that this is happening," Jason stated.

"Yes, and even worse, Dr. Smith helped. It wasn't our fault that the patient died. Our cure had worked, but Dr. Smith injected him with something to mutate the virus and kill the patient."

"They weren't going to help us find a cure," Zachary said.

"What the hell? Smith had something to do with all of this? And he killed that poor old man?" Jason growled. "We needed to find a way to get out of here."

"I know," Zachary said, "but I don't know how."

They started trying to find a way to escape the base, but they weren't having any luck. The base was locked down, and there was no way out. They were running out of time and needed to find a way out soon. They returned to the lab to think.

Just then, Sergeant Lynne came into the lab and said, "I have been thinking about this, and I think I might have a way to get us out of here."

"What is it?" Jason asked.

"I can't tell you yet," Sergeant Lynne said, "but I need your help."

The team decided to trust Lynne and followed him out of the lab. They weren't sure what he had planned, but they were willing to try anything at this point, desperate for the chance of survival. When they got to Sergeant Lynne's room, he opened a hidden panel in the wall and took out a map.

"This is a map of the base," he said.

"I have been planning my escape for a while now."

"Why didn't you just leave?" Jason asked.

"I had my reasons," Sergeant Lynne said, his body language turning more defensive. "But that doesn't matter now."

“Sergeant?” Zachary said, trying to get Sergeant Lynne’s attention.

“Just call me Xavier,” he replied.

“You know it wasn’t your fault, Xavier,” Zachary said, trying to cheer him up.

Jason felt he was missing something but didn’t pressure them to find out.

“I’m Jason,” announced Jason.

“I am Zachary,” Zachary added.

“Might as well use first names; titles are currently irrelevant.”

“So, what was the plan?” Jason asked.

“We need to get to the armory,” Xavier said.

“Why do we need to go there?” Zachary asked.

“I have a plan, but we need some supplies,” Xavier said with a doubtful tone.

“What kind of supplies?” Jason inquired.

“Armor. What the hell did you think we were getting? Swords and chain mail?” Zachary asked sarcastically.

Xavier sighed. "I'll need some explosives, but some guns wouldn't hurt," he said. "And I'll need your help to get them."

They agreed to help him get their needed supplies. Once they arrived, Xavier took out his map again.

"This is where we need to go," he said.

"But how were we going to get past security?" Zachary asked.

"I have a plan for that, too," Xavier said.

They got to the security room. Two guards got ready to shoot when Xavier announced his name as Sergeant Lynne, hoping Major Jameson hadn't updated the system yet.

"You're clear to enter. Those two are not," one of the guards said, still in a ready stance.

"Wait here. I'll be right back," Xavier said, entering the security room.

Xavier came out with a grin, saying, "Okay, all systems looked good. Let's get back to the lab; we should have time to settle things and start working on a cure."

Zachary and Jason were confused but tried not to show it.

"Sounds good," Zachary said and started to walk in the direction of the lab.

They walked a little past the security room and stopped.

"Okay, thanks for keeping cover. I was really hoping you would follow my lead on that. Next is the armory. Let's go right this way," Xavier said, leading them.

The team made their way to the armory. Xavier took out a device that looked hand-made. He attached it to the door.

"This should do the trick," he said as he stepped back, and the team took cover. Xavier activated the device, and there was a loud explosion. The door was blown open, and the team ran into the room. They were still unsure what Xavier had planned, but there was no going back now. They grabbed a couple of bags of weapons and supplies. Xavier led the team to a hidden tunnel that he found on his map.

"This tunnel will take us out of the base," he said.

"But it's going to be dangerous."

"We're ready," Jason said. "Let's go."

His voice echoed through the tunnel as he entered.

Zachary and Jason followed Xavier through the tunnel. It was dark, and they couldn't see where they were going. They were depending on Xavier to get them out safely. The tunnel was long and winding, and the team started to get tired. They kept going because they knew that their survival depended on it. Finally, they saw a light up ahead.

They followed it and noticed that it was a door. Xavier opened it, and they realized that they were outside.

They had made it out of the base safely.

As the team walked away from the base, they realized they needed to find a way to survive in this new world on their own. They didn't know how long they would be out there but needed to find a way to make it. They set up camp and started to gather supplies. They needed to find food and water; they weren't sure what the future held, but they were determined to survive. As night fell, they huddled around the fire and tried to stay warm. They weren't sure what the next day would bring, but they knew that they needed to stick together if they were going to make it.

Infected people were aggressive and, most importantly, agitated by noise at night, so they had to be quiet. Jason was on the lookout while the others tried to get some sleep.

Suddenly, Jason heard something. He woke everyone up and told them to be quiet. He wasn't sure what it was, but he knew it was coming closer. The team prepared for a fight as the noise grew closer and closer. But when other people came into view, the team was shocked to see they weren't alone. Other people were also trying to survive in this new world. The team was relieved to know that they weren't the only ones.

"Friend or foe?" one of the survivors yelled at them.

"Not smart to ask if we're a foe. People who are foes would lie and say 'friend' and then ambush the others," Zachary said sarcastically. "But we are friendly. We were scientists, and Xavier here was military."

The survivors walked closer to the team. There were three of them: a man, a woman, and a child. They looked exhausted and scared but were also relieved to see other people.

"My name is David," the man said.

"This is my wife, Sarah," he pointed to the woman. "And this is our daughter, Emily."

Sarah held up a little girl who couldn't be more than five years old.

"We've been out here for weeks. We were part of a group, but we got separated."

"We've been trying to find our way back to the camp, but we didn't know where it is," Sarah said. "Do you know where it is?"

She looked at Xavier.

Xavier looked at the map. He knew the camp was in this area but wasn't sure where it was.

"I'm not sure," he said. "But I think we can find it."

"We need to find it," Sarah said. "We can't stay out here much longer. We're running out of supplies."

"We'll help you find it," Jason said. "But first, we must find a way to survive out here."

The team and the survivors started to work together. They gathered food and water. They took turns standing watch. It was Xavier's turn to stand watch when he noticed Zachary tossing and turning. He jumped down and woke Zachary up.

"Sorry, it looked like you were having a nightmare," Xavier said.

Zachary replied, "Yeah, between the infected and the kid, I am unsure if they are a good idea to have around. The kid could alert nearby infected or unfriendly people."

"I've been thinking about that. We'll try to find their camp as soon as we can. We won't stay there, not that kids are a problem. They're just a risk I'm not willing to take right now."

Zachary nodded his head, "I just wish we had never come out here."

Xavier put a hand on Zachary's shoulder. "We all do, but we are alive, and that is what counts."

Xavier climbed back into the tree to keep watch as Zachary tried to get some more sleep. But he couldn't shake the feeling that something bad would happen. Morning came without any issues. Birds chirped, and the sun was rising, bathing the horizon in a pink glow. Golden fingers of sunshine illuminated the scene.

"I miss being at peace. It has been a very long time since I felt peaceful." Jason said while looking at the sunrise.

"I know the feeling," Xavier replied.

He climbed down from the tree and walked over to Sarah.

"I will take the first watch," he said.

"Thank you," she said, handing Emily to Xavier, who held her close.

"Be careful," Sarah said.

"We will," Xavier said as he walked away with Emily in his arms. It had been a few weeks since the team and the survivors had found each other. They were slowly making their way toward the camp but were running out of supplies. They had been rationing what they had, but it wasn't enough. The team was getting tired and weak from starvation. The baby cried all the time, and it was driving everyone crazy. Sarah was getting frustrated with Emily.

"I'm sorry," she said.

"I know you are doing your best, but we need to find food and water soon," Jason said comfortingly, trying to keep up the team's morale.

"We'll find something," Xavier said. "We just have to keep looking."

The team kept looking, but they couldn't find anything. They were about to give up when Xavier found a small stream of water. They filled their bottles and drank as much as they could. Then, they followed the stream until they found a small farmhouse. There was a garden out back with some vegetables growing in it. The team started to gather the vegetables and put them in their bags.

They were about to leave when Sarah stopped them.

"Wait," she said. "We can't just take all of this. This is someone's food."

"Sarah, we don't have a choice," Jason said. "We are going to die if we don't eat something soon, and it is probably abandoned anyways."

Sarah looked at the team, realizing they were right. They needed to eat to survive. But she couldn't help but feel guilty about taking someone's food. The team set up camp in the farmhouse. They were exhausted, but they were happy to have food and water.

The next morning, Sarah woke up to the sound of Emily crying. She got up to feed her, but Emily wasn't there. Sarah started to panic as she looked for Emily but didn't see her anywhere. Then she heard a noise coming from the other room. She ran into the room and saw Emily crawling on the floor.

"Emily!" Sarah said as she picked her up.

"I thought I had lost you." Sarah hugged Emily tightly, starting to cry. She was relieved that she was safe but also worried about what could have happened if she hadn't found her.

The infected were everywhere. The team had to be careful as they made their way through the city. They were looking for supplies, but they were also looking for a safe place to rest. The baby was crying again, and Sarah was getting frustrated.

"I can't do this anymore," she said. "We have to find a safe place soon."

Xavier nodded his head and led the team toward a tall building. They went inside and started to look around. It was quiet, and there didn't seem to be any infected around.

"Sarah, David," Xavier called out quietly. They both looked at Xavier concerningly. "This city is surrounded by infected. We are lucky this building seems to be clear, and we are not ready to be attacked. We need to find a way to keep Emily quieter so we don't die out here," Xavier grimly stated.

Emily had been crying for days. They had not had a good night's sleep in weeks.

The infected were attracted to noise. Sarah suggested that they build a crib out of boxes and blankets. Xavier agreed, and they started to work on it. It was not perfect, but it could do.

The team got ready to settle in for the night when they heard a noise outside. They all froze and listened carefully. It sounded like someone was coming toward the building. Sarah grabbed a knife and prepared to defend herself. The door burst open, and a man ran into the room.

"Help me!" he cried. "They're coming!"

The infected were right behind him. Sarah cut the man's throat in a state of panic before he could make any more noise. Then she and the team started to fight the infected storming through the door. It was a bloody battle, but they eventually managed to kill all of the infected. They closed and locked the door but knew it wouldn't hold for long.

"We need to find a way out of here," Sarah said. "We can't stay."

Xavier nodded angrily, and they started to look for a way out. But it was too late. The infected were already inside the building. Sarah and the team were surrounded, and they fought as best they could.

"Zachary, Jason, I have an idea. You may not like it, but trust me. It will save your lives," Xavier shouted.

He picked up Emily and threw her into the horde of infected, distracting them momentarily.

"Daddy!" Emily shouted as the infected started to bite into her flesh.

"Hel–" she tried to call, but one infected bit into her neck, tearing out her throat, her words turning into gurgles as she choked out her last breath.

"You son of a bitch!" David shouted as he turned around, swinging a knife at Xavier and cutting his arm.

"I will kill you!" Sarah shouted. "I trusted you!"

Xavier shoved David into the infected and then grabbed Zachary and Jason, starting to run to the fire escape. He was bleeding badly.

"I know it was wrong, but you guys needed to stay alive. Only you can save humanity," Xavier said weakly.

"A kid, though?" Jason replied.

"That was hard to watch, and I still feel sick."

"We can talk about it later. Let's get to safety first," Xavier replied.

The team was able to get to the bottom of the fire escape, but it did not lead to the ground; the last floor's ladder was broken.

"In here," Xavier pointed. "The doors are stronger than the rest, so we should be able to wait out the infected here."

Everyone agreed and started covering the doors with furniture for extra protection.

"For the record, I do not agree with what you did," Jason said, handing Xavier a first aid kit he found in the bathroom.

"Thank you," Xavier replied tiredly.

The morning had risen, and the infected were still pounding at the door.

"What now?" Jason asked Xavier, who was now resting against the wall covered in blood and sweat.

"I don't know," Xavier replied. "We need a miracle."

Just then, they heard a helicopter in the distance. It was getting closer and closer. The team started to shout and wave their arms. The helicopter saw them and dropped a ladder from the side.

They were saved!

The team climbed into the helicopter, and they were flown to safety. They had survived against all odds. But Xavier knew that this was only the beginning. The fight for humanity had just begun. The infected were everywhere, and the team would have to be careful if they wanted to survive.

Chapter 5: The Savior

The helicopter flew away from the base. They sat across each other, listening to its deafening whirl. While Zachary and Jason took a sigh of relief, Xavier was pensive. He knew that it was the beginning of the beginning. There was still a long way to go. Humanity had to be saved. Pain numbed him, but he tried to remain conscious.

Roger, an ex-marine cop, sat in the front seat with a pilot who remained engrossed in his work. His massive build and tall figure made him look stronger and more serious. He told them he had been assigned a task to save the survivors.

"Thanks, Roger," said Zachary, grateful that this man had saved their life.

"You need to go to a hiding place for some time now. We need supplies for our survival," said Roger, rolling his eyes through the glass of the helicopter.

He looked down to identify areas where clusters of zombies were concentrated.

"Are you going to drop us at the hiding place you are talking about?" Jason asked, turning towards Roger immediately.

"Yes, the virus is everywhere. Almost everyone is infected in every town. You need to keep yourself safe now," Roger said.

He told them the virus had spread far and wide; protecting oneself from the ongoing apocalypse was difficult.

Xavier and Zachary sat silent. They all gave each other concerning looks. None of them knew if they would be safe at the hiding place. Xavier tried not to show the pain he was feeling.

Roger continued, "There is a mall where we can get enough supplies to survive a few days. The zombies attacked it during the outbreak. We are still not sure if the place is free from them. We assume there will be zombies, but we must secure supplies."

"How long will it take us to reach the hiding place from where you're dropping us?" inquired Zachary.

He knew they would encounter Zombies on their way.

Roger replied, "Not much. Fifteen minutes. But you need to be careful on your way. Zombies are roaming all around the town. They might attack if they find you."

After pausing, he continued, "We will wait for you in the helicopter. You need to go and bring the necessary supplies from the mall."

Zachary and Jason shook their heads, having understood. They all sat in silence, pondering over the unpredictability of the situation they would face.

Meanwhile, the helicopter flew towards Baltimore, Maryland. After flying for some time, Roger stood up and threw the ladder. Zachary and Jason stepped down one by one. Xavier was feeling fine now, and the pain had lessened. He went along with the two scientists.

They had arrived in Baltimore. Like every American town, Baltimore had turned into the city of the dead. A deathlike and ghostly silence prevailed there. The huge buildings were empty, and abandoned cars lined up on the roads. The cafes and restaurants that were once vibrant now presented a sanguinary sight. Their walls were covered with blood that had dried. There were no dead bodies, as the virus had turned each of them into zombies. It was shocking and gruesome to them. They had never even imagined that their world would come to a standstill like this.

Without resting, they started walking towards the mall, where they would hide. Xavier guided them as they sauntered toward their targeted place. As the three of them were walking, they heard sounds. They stopped—the sounds of steps getting closer chilled their spine.

"I think there are zombies there," said Jason as fear spread over his facial features.

Through gestures, Zachary asked him to stop talking. He signaled them to stop and wait while he checked the unknown movements around them. The sounds were coming closer. Zachary gave Jason an indication to take care of Xavier. He looked around and saw two humans approaching them. At first, he thought they were zombies and alerted his friends, but then he realized both were, in fact, normal. Zachary was simultaneously shocked and delighted to see that the people approaching them were their old fellows, Kate and Morgan.

He cried in excitement, "Kate! Morgan!"

Jason and Xavier, who were waiting behind him, also saw Kate and Morgan. They hugged each other. Zachary and Jason were happy to see Kate and Morgan alive. Having separated during the breakout, they thought they had died because none of the people they knew were alive when the zombie apocalypse had occurred.

"How did you both get here?" asked Zachary.

"We were stuck in the town. We survived the Zombie attack twice," Kate replied.

She continued reflecting on their experience, "They were very scary, Zachary. I couldn't stand the sight of my friends turning into zombies. Those spasms of the dead! The virus had turned them into beasts. Their rotten flesh, shambling figures, and demonic eyes were gruesome. They made me so hopeless. I thought I would be dead. Then Roger came and saved us. He brought us here."

Morgan added, "He told us we can get supplies here."

Jason and Zachary nodded and seemed hopeless, too, and told them they had been given the same information, too. They also told Kate and Morgan about their encounter with zombies and how swarms of zombies had attacked them.

"When we were told the base would be attacked in two days, we decided to leave it. When we left, we met this small family. However, they came under zombie attack, and we had to leave them behind. There was this small girl, Emily, with them. I can't forget her terrified face," Jason told Kate and Morgan.

They all became silent, realizing the graveness of the situation. Would the world never become normal again? Would all mankind turn into zombies? Would this planet be known as the planet of the dead in history books? Five thousand years from now, will this planet survive? These questions haunted them all, yet they were clueless. Human civilization was under assault, and there was little that they could do about it.

Introducing Xavier to Kate and Morgan and vice versa, Zachary said, "He is sergeant Xavier."

"I hope you people are well," Xavier asked Kate and Morgan.

They replied to him in their half-fainting voice that a zombie had attacked them when they were leaving the town. They all felt sorry but, at the same time, happy to see each other. They started walking towards the mall, which Roger had told them about.

Xavier led the team while Zachary and Kate walked ahead. They looked around vigilantly to see if there were any zombies, and Jason and Morgan followed soon behind.

"We need to be very careful," said Xavier as he walked and kept watch.

Morgan asked, "Do you think zombies are here? This place looks like a dead end. Even zombies would have left."

Zachary replied anxiously, "They are here."

Everyone gave him an uneasy look.

"There is only one way to get rid of this apocalypse—we need to find a cure to kill the mutated virus," said Xavier, the gnawing sensation still in his mind.

Jason replied, looking at all of them, "We need to be quick with that, or this apocalypse will infect us too."

They quickly but watchfully made their way ahead, avoiding making any noise. Zachary, Morgan, and Jason were more afraid than usual. Xavier told them not to panic and that they would get through this.

"Don't worry. We will get to the mall safely."

Meanwhile, they all devised a plan to secure necessary supplies from the mall.

"Firstly, we need a first aid kid and some pain relievers," said Morgan, anxiously looking at their injuries.

Kate told Zachary and Jason, "Morgan and I will bring the kit and pain relievers. You will stay with Xavier."

"Don't worry, you will be fine," Xavier tried hard to comfort people walking along with him.

They all looked at him in distress.

"I am good. We ought to save this world together. We are not dying before that," he said, forcing a smile on his face, but it still revealed his pain.

They smiled back at him.

"We will," replied Jason reassuringly, determination evident in his words.

Xavier could decipher it in an instant.

"We need to find food first. We all will die out of starvation before the zombies find us," Zachary said, looking here and there to see if there was any shop where they could find preserved food.

"I will stay with the sergeant. You search nearby shops to see if the food is available there," Jason told Zachary.

"No, we all must stay together," Xavier replied.

Chapter 6: The Mall

"Have you ever read *Fantastic Mr. Fox* by Roald Dahl? Or watched the movie?" asked Jason as he tossed granola bars into a yellow duffel bag he'd acquired off the rack in Aisle 8.

"Not that I recall, no," replied Xavier.

They had decided to spread out in order to save time. Captain Roger was on standby in the helicopter, and they hadn't been able to assess how long they possibly had until the noise from it drew attention to them.

Once inside the mall, the game plan had been this: Morgan would collect medicine and first aid, Kate would collect water, Zachary would collect clothes, and Xavier would collect hardware equipment. An additional responsibility that Xavier had taken upon himself was to protect the entire gang. But as soon as they'd entered the mall, he'd walked over to the culinary section and handed each of them a butcher's knife.

"It's imperative that you keep a weapon since we've decided to split up. If you need backup, shout your name and your aisle number."

"In *Fantastic Mr. Fox*, three farmers drive out a family of foxes that had been stealing their turkeys, chickens, and cider," said Jason.

“The foxes dig a deep hole underground where they find all the other forest animals and their respective wives and kids. Everyone wants to save themselves, so they dig upwards towards a mall and have an unlimited reservoir of food from that point onwards.”

“That’s exactly what we’re doing now,” said Xavier.

He didn’t chide Jason for trying to make conversation during a time-critical operation; it was important that everyone kept their spirits up and always behaved like a team. That meant giving someone a listening ear, even when they were in deep trouble. Perhaps he was making small talk to calm his nerves, thought Xavier.

“It’s really funny,” commented Jason. He was looking for a bottle of olive oil. The backpack was getting filled with superfoods: non-perishable nutrition that could sustain their daily needs. The yield so far looked like this: boxes of sugar-free wheat biscuits, coconut oil, instant oatmeal, mixed nuts, various types of nut butter, unripe bananas, and – of course – the granola bars. He also tossed in a few plastic jars of honey.

Xavier had acquired ropes, grappling hooks, a claw hammer and mallet, a screwdriver set, a socket wrench set, pliers, and even a laptop computer and smartphone. He carried this in a black duffel that he was now carrying on his back.

At the other end of the mall, Kate was hauling water bottles into her lot of duffels. She'd already filled up four.

A few aisles down, Morgan was filling his backpack with sanitary napkins, soap, and first aid. The haul was not methodical for anyone; they meant to get this over with this within five minutes.

Zachary was alone on the first floor. It was darker here than downstairs, but he could see alright. He was running from clothing store to store, grabbing T-shirts, jeans, gloves, caps, socks, and underwear. He stopped by a small Nike store and let out an audible gasp of relief. They would need a pair of closed boots each and a pair of shoes that were easy to run in.

He walked into the store and marched towards the All-Stars on display by the wall. It smelled putrid here, and he wondered if someone shat themselves. *Never mind*, he thought as he reached out to grab the first pair of sneakers to toss into his ba—

Something shifted at the counter on his right.

Too terrified to turn around, Zachary feebly convinced himself that it had been his imagination and quickened the pace of his work.

But out of the corner of his eye, he saw a small figure reach up and thump the counter. It was a rotting hand. The hand was attached to a rotting body. The rotting body had, obviously, stank. And it was now in his full field of vision.

Zachary should have never come here in the first place.

"*AAAAAAAAAAAAAAAAHHHHH*!" he screamed, turning around and darting towards the door.

"Aaaaaaaaaaaah," replied the zombie in inadvertent mimicry but in a voice that was decidedly hoarse and dead.

It started walking towards him. Zachary spun his head around to see the zombie confidently trudging towards him – he'd almost definitely been a business associate or lawyer, given the self-assurance with which he proceeded his languid chase.

Zachary wondered why on earth the movies made it seem like they could outrun them.

"ZACHARY, FIRST FLOOR CORRIDOR TO THE RIGHT!" barked Zachary when he remembered the protocol.

Downstairs, everyone had convened. They cocked their heads up at the shouting.

Xavier was the first to speak.

"You three, head outside and get in the chopper."

"No, we want to stay with you," said Jason.

"You're carrying too many things. Go to the chopper!" he had made it halfway toward the stairs by then.

Kate looked at Jason and Morgan and said, "We have to cover them, right? He can't fight them all alone."

"Yeah, let's drop these bags by the entrance, and then we can go help out," agreed Jason.

They darted to the front of the entrance, flung their bags off their shoulders and arms, and hurled them in one swooping motion towards it. The bags collided against the sliding doors in a huge mound, and there was a small crash. The doors whooshed open and froze as the bags stimulated the motion sensor by the sill. The sound of the chopper grew louder tenfold and roared through the entire mall.

"ZACHARY, FIRST FLOOR TURNING TO A CORRIDOR AT FOUR O'CLOCK FROM ZARA." Zachary bellowed.

When Xavier heard this, he realized how much better this call for backup would have worked if there were just aisle numbers. Why had he overlooked this?! He scanned his surroundings anxiously but failed to see a Zara store.

"I'm here, Zach!" he yelled. "Where are you from, Sketchers?"

"I DON'T KNOW WHERE SKETCHERS IS FOR FLIP'S SAKE. THERE IS A DEAD GUY ON MY TAIL!"

Xavier took a deep breath and readjusted his pistol, which he had removed from his holster as soon as he'd heard the first scream.

"I think I heard you on the right side!" he called out.

"XAVIER, HE'S GAINING ON ME."

"So just outrun him!"

"XAVIER, THEY ARE VERY SMART!"

Xavier started sprinting towards the right, where he was certain Zachary was yelling from. He hadn't been able to tell at first; the sound of the chopper had gotten much louder – it was already louder on the first floor – but now, he had attuned his ears to the noise enough to be able to parse through it and assess Zachary's direction.

Kate and Jason appeared from behind a wall in front of him.

"Where did you come from, and what are you guys doing here?!" Zachary said.

"The stairs," said Jason, pointing towards a set from behind the wall where they'd appeared.

"We're not going to let you go through this alone."

"Guys, I appreciate the --- ah, alright, come on! You've got your weapons?"

"XAVIER!" yelled Zachary with all his life.

He tripped on a loose tile and fell.

Before he could pick himself up, the zombie arrived at his heels. The stench grew stronger, and the rot grew horrider. Zachary's stomach lurched uncomfortably. The creature was unbearable to witness.

Here, the sound of the chopper was deafening.

Zachary squeezed his eyes shut.

It wasn't as though the zombie had been unable to catch up with him during the wild goose chase that had just unfolded. It was that the zombie knew he could catch up and didn't need to sweat it because he was a dangerous creature of the undead that had been made to seem more innocuous than it really was.

The zombie hadn't followed Zachary around because it needed to. The zombie was simply working up its appetite like a cat playing with its food.

Zachary whispered a silent prayer for his cat Silo who he'd lost when he was six. It was the last thing he wanted to think about.

The putrid stench grew stronger and stronger until he could feel the death that emanated from it. It was cold and gruesome and incoming. It felt as though death was vacuuming him – a gravitational force field of extinction that was paradoxically cold. Zachary put his elbows up in a last gesture of defense. And then it splatted on top of him. The motionless creature felt pasty somehow. Something had thumped and rolled over to his right.

Zachary grimaced and opened his eyes in disgust.

"Let's go!" said Morgan over the sound of the rotors outside. He was holding a sword that dripped some sort of dark grey sap.

Zachary pushed the dead weight on his body to a side. It was headless. It oozed the same rotting grey sap.

"Ugh!" cringed Zachary as he wiped it off his neck. He followed Morgan to the end of the corridor where the rotor sounds were coming from. A shattered glass window within the wall stood between them and the helicopter.

Just then, the others arrived.

"Hi!" shouted Captain Rogers.

The others smiled. Zachary looked wounded.

"You guys getting out of here or what? It's been sixteen minutes!"

The rotor chopped viciously.

"We're getting the—"

There was a loud, gruesome splat as grey sap flew in every direction– onto the shattered glass pane, on the faces and profiles of everyone standing there, on the walls around them, on the floor in front of them, and on the polished concrete outside.

Captain Rogers had only felt a large thump above that destabilized the chopper slightly and seen the rivulets that rained down the windscreen ahead of him. But what had actually happened was this: a morbidly obese rotting human body deliberately had jumped off the roof of the building, fallen directly on the chopper's rotors, and been diced immediately.

The rotor whirled emphatically to rid itself of the oozing sap. It was an altogether disgusting sight.

"What the fuck?!" exclaimed Kate.

"It jumped off the roof. Guys, get to the exit. I'll turn this around," said Captain Rogers, closing a fist around the cyclic control.

The group collectively roared and ran. They raced down the corridor, down the stairs, and towards the entrance, which they were also using as an exit point.

Only Morgan and Zachary had encountered a zombie before, but the rest of the group was smart enough to figure out where the sap had come from. The stench left no room for speculation.

But Xavier was the first to realize that this order of procession was probably not the best of ideas. It seemed that they understood nothing about their enemy. Zachary had said they were smart. But then, one of them had jumped off a building directly into a chopper's blades. It was as though it had been attracted to the sound. It didn't seem like an intelligent thing to do.

They were truly in a war zone: volatile, hostile, and unpredictable. If they wanted to stop running amok every time they encountered a zombie, Xavier and the gang would have to take stock and conduct a rigorous SWOT analysis.

"Guys – guys!" he said when the group darted ahead towards the final aisles leading to the exit.

They stopped, hesitantly turned around, and looked at him intently.

Xavier hesitated too, but then said, "Make sure you have your weapons on you. Let's go!"

The group nodded, checked that they were armed, and then proceeded toward the entrance.

It was radio silent. Their mound of supplies was still stationed at the center of the almost-all-the-way-through open doorway.

They walked up quickly to the entrance, and each person picked up at least two duffels; at least two slung around everyone's backs and another protecting their vitals on the front. Xavier said that their backpacks were like armor, but they felt extremely heavy.

Xavier, who had been leading the way throughout the process, turned around and brought a finger to his lips.

"Ssssh!" he said, making it doubly clear that they were supposed to stay quiet.

"We move as one unit. No falling out," he said, raising his voice slightly.

They organized themselves into a unit and arranged their weapons such that each person held them toward the outside. In this way, they were impenetrable, totally fortified organisms.

They stationed themselves at an approximate distance of one foot apart from each other so as to ensure that there was no shuffling.

So these five people and over twenty duffel bags full of supplies crept out of the threshold.

It was very sunny outside. The parking lot was totally clear. Ahead of them, they could hear the whir of a chopper growing louder as it approached—

"Boo!" yelled a zombie, which had sprung out from behind a landscaping potter ahead of them. In sharp contrast to the vitality of its actions, the zombie's voice was, once more, hoarse and dead.

"Aaah!" screamed everyone in unison.

And then, hoards of zombies approached from either side of the building from which the group had just emerged.

Xavier, at the front, was the first one to snap out of it. He brought up his butcher's knife and dug it into the zombie's head before him. The weight of duffel bags contributed to the force of the blow, and he managed to slice the zombie all through its center. It fell apart in two different directions.

Meanwhile, the others had turned backward and readied themselves into defensive positions.

Xavier felt that they were losing the element of ambush, which the zombies had ingeniously applied, but could see that the zombies were probably unperturbed. The group was hopelessly outnumbered.

The zombies were approaching them in swarms. Before his eyes, all-out warfare broke out. Kate and Jason manned eleven and one o'clock, swishing their knives violently at the zombies – chopping heads, limbs, eyeballs, what have you.

At eight, nine, three, and four o'clock, Morgan and Zachary made second, fatal strikes on the zombies that were still left.

But the zombies had closed in on them such that the group couldn't move. They were a writhing, twisting organism amid a sea of the undead. And they were fighting for their life.

The helicopter hovered above them, and Captain Rogers let down a ladder of rope. Xavier placed a foot on the first step and raised his foot for the second when he realized that the rope couldn't hold the weight of him and the three duffel bags. Keeping one hand firmly on the rope, he forcefully dislodged two bags with the other. Xavier felt devastated. The supplies would have made things much more convenient, but then he thought that they'd been fools to fill up such large bags when there were, in fact, only six of them in all.

"Jason," he yelled. "Climb!"

Jason struck his knife against a zombie's head and spun his head back and up.

He grabbed Morgan by the arm, who was flailing wildly about and slitting zombies wherever he could, and moved a couple of steps back to the chopper.

"Lose the duffels!" yelled Xavier.

"What?"

"They're too heavy. DROP THEM!"

Jason dropped one. Then, he quickly climbed up the ladder, but not before turning Morgan around and stationing him to climb up right after him.

"Kate! Zach!" yelled Xavier. He was fighting off the zombies that were trying to climb.

The bodies of zombies had almost swallowed them whole, and the two fought hard to keep them off. Kate wished they had more backup. She took a couple of steps back and tried to search for Morgan's hand with her own. It felt like wading through thick, cold waters. But it was impossible to do so while still fighting off the zombies.

"Hey!"

It was a strange man's voice. Kate and Morgan could not see beyond the zombies that had enveloped them, but at a height of a foot and a half, Xavier watched a crowd of people emerge from within the mall's entrance.

They carried a motley bunch of armaments: baseball bats, swords, knives, lamps – what have you.

And they launched themselves directly at the zombies.

Chapter 7: The Bait for Dead

Xavier opened his eyes and blinked. Complete darkness surrounded him. He wondered where the others had brought him and why it was dark. Were they in hiding? He didn't remember climbing the helicopter. The last thing he remembered was reaching out to grab Kate with a hand gripped around Zachary's forearm. He blinked again, trying to adjust his eyes to the darkness.

"Hello?" he heard a familiar voice behind him.

It was Zachary.

"Zach!" he exclaimed, relieved, "Where are we?"

Silence. Why wasn't he responding?

"Zach?" said Xavier, his voice trembling slightly. A sharp pain exploded on the right of his head. He tried reaching it with his hand but realized his arms were tied up behind him.

"HEY, WHAT THE HELL?!" Xavier bellowed and immediately regretted it.

He felt weak and close to fainting. He couldn't remember the last time he'd eaten or even drunk some water, and thinking about it strained his mind.

"You were passed ou—" Kate's voice, echoing somewhere in the darkness, was cut short by the sound of heavy footsteps.

"Kate? Kate!" Xavier said.

The footsteps approached closer. And suddenly, he was blinded by the light. A pair of jeaned legs stood beside him. The owner wore cargo boots. He looked up and saw a white circle of light, which he recognized as a flashlight bulb when his eyes adjusted themselves. A shadowy figure hung above it.

The only thing that Xavier could feel was terror.

"*Ay, tu conveghi*?"

The voice was also female but deeper and more hostile than Kate's. It echoed ominously.

"What the hell is happeni—"

She kicked him in the arm. It didn't hurt as much as it humiliated him.

"*Ghesponthma!*" the creature exclaimed, "*Ay, tu conveghi*?"

Xavier maintained his silence.

"*Bien.*"

The woman turned around and flashed a light at Kate. She was tied by the arms to a white pillar. Xavier's eyes widened in shock, but he refused to speak.

"Wait," said another familiar voice. It was Captain Roger.

Captain Roger, thought Xavier, relieved. He wondered if these people had hijacked the chopper and brought the group to a strange location.

Captain Rogers was straining to speak.

"Miss, you have the wrong crowd here. We have – done you no harm. We're simply – simply – trying to escape this group of zombies."

"*Ay, tu conveghi?*"

Xavier heaved an audible gasp of relief and realization. This was a Frenchwoman. She was asking if they were converted. Only '*Es-tu converti*' had sounded like possible zombie jargon in his groggy head.

He had taken a few French courses in undergrad and was rusty since, but he could still understand the gist of it.

"No! No!" Xavier yelled.

The flashlight turned to him once again. He wrinkled his eyes to shield them.

"We are not converted! We are not zombies!"

He tried to enunciate every syllable in the hopes that she would understand. The woman said nothing but left. The group quietly listened to her footsteps fade away. They disappeared into a height – some sort of ramp north of where Xavier was tied up.

"Captain!" said Xavier, "What's going on here?"

He tried to turn his head but realized it was of no use; he couldn't see where the Captain was anyway.

"You got bludgeoned on the head real bad," said Zachary bitterly.

"These people that we thought were here to rescue us beat up the zombies but then arrested us. We were brought over here at gunpoint, and a man in the group carried you. Captain said–"

"Captain! Where's the chopper?" said Xavier.

There was an uncomfortable silence.

"Captain asked Morgan and the others to drive off when he saw the group arresting us. He tried to talk to them, but they tazed him and brought him over here."

"What the fuck?" said Xavier. His head was spinning. "Where are we? The basement of the mall?"

"Yes," said Captain Rogers.

"How many of these people are there?"

"At least fifty. My estimation is that they were hiding in the basement."

"What basement?"

"*This* basement, where we currently are. There are some quilts laid out where I am."

"WE'RE STILL IN THE MALL?!"

"Shush! They beat up most of the zombies, but others are still out there. And they are *smart*. We need to keep quiet," said Zachary. "These people obviously have, for a very long time."

"What do they want from us?" said Xavier. He couldn't believe this.

Zachary refused to respond.

"Have you told them that we're not zombies?"

"They know. I showed them my badge," said Captain Rogers. He sounded dejected. "They're keeping us here as zombie bait."

"*What?!*" said Xavier, "Is there no way that we can escape?"

He started writhing viciously. It only seemed to tighten the knots.

"It's a pretty hopeless situation."

"We have to put our heads together!" screamed Xavier, "I did not come this far only to be fed voluntarily to zombies!"

There was silence again. It appeared that the whole group was resigned to its fate.

"I am having none of this!" Xavier said firmly. His head hurt terribly. "And the medicine? The supplies?"

"They took all of it," Zachary said weakly.

They heard a series of sounds. It was the same heavy footfall of the cargo boots.

"*Je vais tous vous libérer si vous promettez d'avoir,*" said the woman in a heavy French accent as her figure approached.

I'm going to release you all provided that you cooperate, Xavier translated her words in his head.

"Merci," he said. There was hope, after all. "Merci beauc—"

His premature gratitude was viciously cut short by the loud boom of a gunshot. Something – blood, flesh – splattered and squelched.

Zachary felt a few droplets on his face. He wrinkled his face because he could not wipe them. The woman dropped in a heap to the floor.

"Nobody is saving anybody!" a man said.

Now that his eyes had adjusted to the dark, Xavier could make this new figure out in the distance. A few feet ahead of him lay the crumpled body of the woman who had to set them free. The man replaced the gun in a holster on his belt and marched back to the basement exit from where he had emerged.

"It's a total shitshow," said Captain Rogers.

"It was nice knowing you all," said Zachary.

Kate simply began to whimper and weep.

***

An inestimable amount of time later, they heard the basement gate open. It released a blinding yellow light from the headlamps of a large vehicle. The truck whirred in their direction.

The doors opened in unison, and four tall, muscular men clambered out of them together. Their discipline indicated to Xavier that they might be military folk.

"I'm armed forces, too!" Xavier exclaimed quixotically.

One of the men looked at him. His eyes were cold and ruthless.

"Good for you, champ," he said. "Use that out there."

Xavier's denial had neither ceded nor ceased.

"You're setting us free!" he exclaimed. "Zach! Kate! They're setting us free."

The group didn't respond to this and merely removed the imprisoned from the pillars. They gripped them and used the same rope to tighten their knots.

Captain Rogers groaned. He had attempted to assault his captor, but the large, steel-built man kicked him in the shin.

Captain Rogers crumpled to the floor, and the man began kicking him in the chest. Each blow further removed whatever little hope remained inside the captain, which he had summoned to attempt to defend himself.

Kate and Zachary were already in the vehicle. Their mouths had been tied up.

Zachary reassured Xavier as his assigned soldier tied up his mouth. All he could manage was a look, but Xavier understood it and climbed into the jeep. The door was shut behind him. The other guard, having fully deflated the captain, tossed him behind them.

Two of the soldiers climbed into the jeep. They took the driver's and passenger's seats. The jeep reversed and then ascended the basement to the parking lot outside. The other two shut the gate.

Once they got into the parking lot, the soldiers climbed out of their seats and hauled the group out.

They tossed them on the parking lot floor. Xavier and Zachary exchanged another look. Kate shivered on the cold concrete. Captain Rogers wasn't even moving. Xavier would have to check if he was breathing.

The soldiers climbed back into the jeep and drove back into the basement. Zachary watched the basement door open and swallow the jeep whole. Then, it shut.

The whole thing couldn't have lasted more than five minutes, but it was the most horrifying of their lives so far. They had been abandoned by the only humans they'd come across ever since the apocalypse broke out.

The moon shone above them. It was brighter here than in the basement.

But there was no silver lining. They were out in the open among the undead.

Zachary looked at Xavier and exchanged another look that meant only one thing: they needed to untie themselves. Captain Rogers was in a complete slump, and Kate had begun whimpering again. They didn't have any of their bearings; Xavier would have to reach into his back pocket and search for a sharp object. He wriggled and squirmed. The tip of his finger brushed against the rugged seams of his pocket, but he could not get them inside. Zachary saw him struggling and tried to wriggle closer to him. Their feet were tied up.

Xavier cast Zachary a discouraging look. He didn't want all of them to attempt the same thing; it would only waste time. They needed to diversify their methods.

He raised his tied fists to his mouth and exhaled, "Mboi!"

Zachary understood the command and inhaled sharply. It pulled the cloth into his mouth, and he began to gnaw at it.

The fabric wettened.

Kate saw what Zachary was doing and imitated the action. Captain Rogers was still not moving.

From somewhere far in the night, the group heard a loud, horrifying shriek. It was deep and throaty and didn't sound human at all.

At that point, everyone in the group - except for Captain Rogers, who was likely unconscious - had a collective epiphany: the creatures out there weren't just zombies or an undead clan that was out to get them. And the people inside hadn't dispelled them for fear of being harmed or simple cruelty. The group had been presented as an offering. These people idolized the zombies; as long as they were well-fed, the group could survive in the basement. This group was a bargain for the others' safety.

Chapter 8: The Rescue

The group – or at least those of them who were awake – continued to gnaw at their respective mouth-ties. The fabric wettened but refused to tear. It was a carefully selected polyester blend. Zachary wondered how many times these people had made offerings to be able to achieve this level of strategic accuracy. But this could be attributed to their military training or a high level of intelligence.

The zombies were very intelligent, too. Zachary shivered to think about how the zombie chased him down the mall and how slow and deliberate it had been with its actions: calm, composed, and self-assured. He thought about the strategic suicide of the other one, that which had trapped them in the parking lot.

He began to gnaw faster. If the zombies got here before everyone present could move their limbs, they would be dead within seconds... or taken away for whatever slow, painful alternative there was.

But no amount of grinding his teeth would create a tear in the fabric, which was more than half its consistency in plastic.

Xavier's ties, on the other hand, had loosened a bit. He had expanded himself into his full form when his captor had been tying him up. This meant that when he shrank himself later, the rope would loosen slightly. He would have more room to wiggle. His hands, however, were firmly tied up. And his head ached terribly.

He reached into his back pocket, lodging a finger into the seam. He strained himself to *reach, reach*, *reach*... and finally got it into the pocket. He moved his finger to check the pocket. It brushed against a piece of paper but failed to yield any sharp object. He tried the other one.

No luck.

Xavier looked around. A rectangular concrete planter was placed a few feet behind him. He sat upright and began to move towards it. He had no idea what they would do once he freed himself but reminded himself to take one step at a time.

Captain Rogers groaned. Everyone looked at him. The slump that he was crumpled into moved. Zachary shushed him. Both he and Kate were following Xavier to the planter. These two had to wiggle because their knots were much tighter.

Xavier pushed himself backward with his hips and feet. The concrete was rough and created friction at the seat of his pants. There was only silence around them, which was just as horrifying as the shriek they'd heard earlier. Out in the open, anything could happen to them, and they were all utterly defenseless with one man partly down.

Xavier looked back. The planter was still a few feet away; he'd covered a little over half the distance.

Zachary pushed his feet and began to roll. He arrived at the planter. After exhaling a sigh at his stupidity, Xavier lay down and did the same while Kate followed suit.

He folded his elbows at the planter, brought them up to his chest, and tightened his hands into fists. There was only a short gap between them, but he began to bring it down – and the rope that held it – onto the planter's edge.

Zachary and Kate watched his swinging motion and attempted to emulate it, but their respective ties were much tighter, and the concrete edge grazed their hands instead.

They heard a mechanical groan from inside the basement door and stopped; if someone came out here and caught them trying to free themselves, they would be delivered directly to the zombies.

Xavier began to perspire heavily. The night blew a breeze in his direction that felt cold against his sweat. He brought his fists down to the concrete, blow after blow, in an effort to cut. He pushed the piece of rope against it and began grinding it.

It required a lot of force, and he had to sit up – and still – in a very uncomfortable position in order to complete this exercise.

The wind started getting stronger. Strands of Kate’s blonde hair blew away from her face. Their clothes began to flutter. And then it stopped.

Probably an oncoming storm, thought Xavier and continued working.

In the distance, a creature convened with others. They knew that the offering was out: the signal, a red light flashed at the top of the mall, had been given. They simply needed to go and collect them.

The zombies began to move. They exited their dilapidated shacks – rooms that they'd acquired through the blunt use of force and murder, feasting on the former residents for weeks.

Xavier could barely see now that the moonlight was cloaked in a cloud, but he kept on grinding. The others had given up entirely. They had resigned themselves to their fate.

Captain Rogers was awake now and had wiggled closer to them. He had accepted an imminent death for them but wanted his last few moments with them.

Then, they heard a footfall. Xavier froze. He heard another groan from the basement and figured the soldiers had come to check on them. Xavier turned around and lay down.

So, this was it. This was how he would come to pass. After all this time and effort, he had been unable to save himself. He had been unable to save the others, which was infinitely more important.

He closed his eyes.

The black changed into orange as a flashlight cast its beams into his eyes.

"Guys!" said a friendly voice in the distance.

Kate let out a muffled garble. Xavier opened his eyes.

Jason and Morgan were darting towards them, both carrying flashlights in their hands.

Xavier could have wept with joy. Morgan caught up with them first. He looked at Captain Rogers and flinched.

"What the hell happened here?" he said.

Zachary exclaimed in outrage, a sound garbled by the cloth in his mouth. He held up his roped fists and looked hard at Jason and Morgan.

"Of course," said Jason and began untying him. Morgan untied Captain Rogers in the meanwhile. He sat him up and leaned his back against the planter.

"Are you okay, Captain?" he said, bending down and leaning close to his face.

Zachary untied Kate as soon as he was free. Jason began to untie Xavier.

Then, they heard a series of rustles. It felt like something was being dragged.

Feet.

The zombies were approaching.

"Let's go!" said Xavier and immediately readied himself for a sprint.

"Where are the supplies?" said Morgan.

"We lost 'em, but no worries. We can raid some other store. Let's *go*!"

"Dude, we have no idea where to find another superstore. We'll die if we don't at least have the basics," Jason said, backing up his partner.

The dragging was getting closer.

***

Kate crept stealthily along the aisles. She dropped some bottles of water into a duffel and then ransacked a shelf of non-perishable foods. The duffel bag was filled with a motley assortment of biscuits and cereal.

She hauled it over her shoulder and proceeded to the other aisle. She grabbed whatever she could: laundry detergent, soap, shampoo – she was sweating profusely and didn't have time to think.

A bottle fell from the aisle and crashed. Kate exhaled sharply and looked around. She needed to be quiet –

The sound of a gunshot pierced the air. A hoarse groan and a series of similar shots followed it. Kate broke into a sprint and tossed whatever she could into the second bag.

She hauled it over her shoulder and made for the makeshift exit: a clerestory window on the first floor. She almost tripped on the motionless escalator and glanced down to see an untied shoelace.

She broadened her gait and continued running.

Xavier leaned an arm over the window, and she tossed a duffel to him. He hauled it up, pulling the heavy bag outside with all his strength. Then, he reached back for the other one.

Kate paused for a moment. She examined the height of the wall and realized that this would seal her exit. She put the duffel bag up against the wall – vertically and at full height.

Then, she lodged the front of her foot into the short strap on top and grabbed Xavier's hand with both of hers.

"Pull," she said, and Xavier did.

He released his pistol and grabbed Kate by the forearms. Now, at least, her head was out of this tiny window. They both pulled her up – Xavier boosting her at the arms and she propelling herself forward with her elbows.

The bag dangled precariously from her foot.

Kate wiggled forward, keeping her foot straight so as not to let the strap escape. She was now horizontally on the ground. Xavier crouched beside her and dislodged the duffel from her foot. He pulled it up, and she straightened, immediately closing the latched window behind her.

The two darted towards the parking lot, where Morgan and Zachary were walking on their side of Captain Rogers. He was weak and bloody. He dragged his feet on the ground, not wholly unlike the zombies that Jason was shooting at.

Four of them lay collapsed in the parking. Jason was shooting at the last two.

Luckily, the zombies had not sent a swarm. They had thought that they wouldn't need much man or zombie power since their offering was tied up.

Even outnumbered, they had been outmaneuvered. Xavier thought that it was pure luck.

"That way!" Morgan pointed towards the right of the mall.

They began moving towards the helicopter, hurrying as much as they could with Captain Roger's injuries and hoping that the humans wouldn't exit the basement to inquire about the source of the gunshots.

Chapter 9: Massacre in the Barracks

They clambered into the chopper one by one, with Zachary and Morgan helping the captain aboard. Jason and Kate heaved the duffel bags inside, and Xavier climbed into the driver's seat.

He was the only one fit for the job. As he powered on the machine, the rotors began to let out a deafening roar. They would have to hurry out of here in order to escape the zombies.

So far, they did not have reason to believe that the zombies had access to vehicles – both on the ground and up in the air – but given the kind of cunning intellect they were dealing with, it wouldn't be wise to rule out the possibility of this altogether.

"Any thoughts on where we're headed, people?' called out Xavier to the back of the chopper as it began its ascent.

Morgan felt that they should keep hovering or roaming around until they found a place, but this would have been unsustainable; the chopper would eventually need to be refueled and, given the dearth of resources as well as their ability to locate various sites, it would be wisest to have a destination in mind.

The hometowns of all of these people were completely out of the question. They had been plagued as soon as the virus had spread out.

They couldn't go to a mountainous range or far out into an island by the sea. And, in a forest, they would have to be on alert against the wild.

They needed to be close enough to civilization so that they could receive help when it survived and far enough so that looters, pillagers, and zombies wouldn't attack them.

Xavier eventually began to panic. They had been in the air for forty minutes with no sense of direction, and the group had, so far, been unable to give an idea that wasn't corroded with loopholes.

"Wake up the captain," he finally said, his tone barely concealing his irritability.

Captain Rogers had his eyes closed. Morgan and Kate had tended to his wounds with whatever first aid Kate had been able to get her hands on, but they had also encouraged him to rest.

"I'm awake, you idiot," he said groggily.

The panic that Xavier had been feeling drained out of him immediately. He grinned.

"I've been trying to evaluate what we can do, and the best that I've come up with so far is that we can head to the barracks," he said, "We'd be armed and in familiar territory. Also, I know how to track the barracks from here. We should be there in another hour."

Captain Rogers mumbled directions at Xavier. He looked and sounded terribly exhausted, and Zachary marveled at the strength of his spirit. The way that he was keeping himself together despite his exhaustion and injury was truly remarkable.

Captain Rogers caught his expression.

"It's the military training," he said humbly and turned his face away.

The landscape below them began to turn dry. They could no longer see buildings and houses but rather a vast expanse of dirt and trees. A single road snaked through the landscape and led out front into the hills.

The Captain was sitting up now. Kate gazed out of the window. She marveled at how incredibly her life had changed within such a short span of time. *One should always be prepared for the unexpected*, she thought.

Morgan had been writing a research paper that would help him get into postgraduate school. He wanted to study and practice medicine. Now, life had put all of that on hold. He also thought that he was fortunate to be with this group of people because, anywhere else, he would have likely been in constant danger. Everyone here had shown constant loyalty to the team and collaborated with one another so far. He felt that they had also lucked out in terms of the strengths of everyone in the group; Captain Rogers and Xavier were military men, Kate was nifty and athletic, and Zachary was intelligent, light-spirited, and helpful.

If they played at each other's strengths, they might just be able to survive.

The group spoke little among themselves on the journey to the barracks; everyone was worn out by the constant stream of events they had endured over the past day and wanted to rest.

Even so, all of them felt alert. The extreme circumstances they'd faced had activated fight-or-flight in all of their brains, which meant that they were doing better than it was, truthfully, plausible to do.

As Zachary realized this, he wondered if the zombies had such sophisticated neural response systems as them. And then he felt himself drift off.

He was awakened by the sound of the descent. The sun had climbed up on the horizon, and the world was gloriously lit. They were surrounded by a vast expanse of dry earth interspersed with green and, sometimes, faded shrubs.

Everyone breathed a sigh of relief as they landed in the chopper strip near the barracks. Captain Rogers was the only one who suspected that something was wrong.

"Shush," he said, looking cautiously at the group behind him, "We need to be careful."

They began to trudge silently toward the barracks. Their hearts raced with apprehension.

Xavier, leading the group, was the first one to see it.

"Oh no," he groaned quietly and turned around.

Captain Rogers picked up speed and limped quickly forward. Beyond the wall that barricaded the site was the scene of a recent carnage.

Bodies were scattered about everywhere: on the sacks of gunpowder and on the ground. They poked out of doorways and over the windows. The bodies, drenched in blood, had belonged to military officials. Their uniform betrayed them.

Flies hovered maliciously everywhere.

"We can't go there," said the Captain, returning to the group. He wanted to spare the others the details, but Xavier had already updated them.

The sun suddenly seemed to grow hotter and more uncomfortable.

"Where else can we go?" asked Kate. She tried to summon hope; they had made it through a dark night of despair not even eight hours ago. All hope had been abandoned, and then a solution had unfurled. Surely, there must be a way out even now.

"Wait," said Captain Roger, "I know another place."

He looked at Xavier, who understood.

"Follow us," said Captain Roger, and the group began to walk behind them.

Chapter 10: The Guilt

Captain Roger was leading the screw to a cabin that he knew of nearby. As a military man, he only underestimated the rest of the group's marching abilities. The cabin was three miles away. It didn't seem like a lot to him and Xavier, but the rest of the group was exhausted.

They tried not to complain but frequently stopped to chug down water on the way. Zachary, who was getting irritated by the stop-and-refuel regime, bit back his tongue. The last they needed in this dire situation was vitriol and consequent altercations among themselves. They needed to stick together as a team, even if that meant slowing down.

Captain Roger and Xavier felt the same way but attempted to temper their annoyance. The captain, still limping slightly, braced himself and kept moving forward. His best service to the group now would be to continue to move. Morgan attempted to help, but the captain asked him to watch out for Kate. She had sprained her ankle during an ascent and needed more looking-after than him.

The group's collective irritation was a disguise for outrageous alarm; they were out in the open during a zombie apocalypse against an enemy they knew nothing about.

Zachary and Xavier tried to temper their anger by taking on more of the load: they each carried a duffel bag. Zachary decided to also contribute by striking up a lighthearted conversation with everyone while they walked.

Jason looked at him discouragingly.

"Don't," he said, "I know you're trying to help, but it's not going to work for now."

They continued to march forward. The sun was blazing hot and blaring directly at them. The whole group was sweating profusely and panting for breath. Being up in the mountains made the exertion much more difficult.

Jason stopped to sprinkle some water over his head to help him cool down.

"We need to stop stopping," Jason said, finally verbalizing what the others had been thinking all this while.

"Don't," said Zachary.

It sounded like mockery just then, and Zachary, quickly realizing this, patted Jason's shoulder with a smile.

Jason understood the gesture and nodded at him. The group continued to march.

"How much farther, Captain?" asked Morgan.

"It isn't much far from here," Captain Roger said, looking back at him.

"Captain," said Xavier quietly, "I have a feeling that we're headed in the wrong direction."

"Where do you think it is?" asked the Captain.

"I think we need to move further northeast."

They discussed it privately among themselves but then decided against splitting up.

In the end, the group had to walk an extra mile and a half before they finally found the cabin. The sun was low by then, and the day had gotten cooler.

A light breeze tickled the trees around the cabin, more and more of which they'd seen as they approached. The change in terrain had been what confirmed the route.

Though shabby and dilapidated, this cabin was a relief for every person in the group. They actually broke into a run toward it as soon as they caught sight of it.

Captain Roger smiled as he approached it. Kate, limping alongside him, exchanged with him an expression of gladness.

The group settled into the cabin for the night. There was no door, but at least it was shelter. A few moldy sofas lay in the living room. The kitchen and bedroom were rusty, cobwebbed, and bare.

Zachary told everyone that it was a good thing the cabin looked so bad and that even Xavier and Captain Roger had had trouble finding it, indicating that it was truly remote and, therefore, difficult to find.

After settling in as comfortably as possible, given the circumstances, the group unpacked the duffel bags and shared a meal.

"What are we going to do about the chopper?" asked Jason as he sipped his coffee. Since they hadn't had any hot water, he'd made this drink by adding coffee beans to a small bottle of water and shaking it. He had volunteered to be on watch tonight. Morgan would be accompanying him. He was also drinking the makeshift coffee.

"I think we should ditch it," said Xavier, "What do you think, Captain?"

The Captain had his leg stretched over the length of the sofa. It was badly bruised. "It would be difficult to refuel it, but aerial transport is definitely safer. We don't know whether the zombies have access to any choppers or aerial vehicles yet."

"I wouldn't rule it out," said Zachary. He told them about his encounter with the zombie at the mall and how incredibly smart and deliberate it had been.

"It appears that these people – I mean, zombies – are made somehow smarter by the virus," commented Kate.

She was huddled in a blanket that smelled of stale water.

"There's a possibility of that," said Jason. He began to explain how, scientifically, the genetic mutation that this virus caused was severely under-researched despite it having been around for a while.

"Why do you think they didn't explore it despite it having been a threat for so long?" asked Jason.

"These people will only research fields that get funded more lucratively," Foster said, leaning back against the sofa.

"And are easier to get funding for," said Zachary.

Jason gave him an appreciative look. "Zach and I were trying to secure a grant to research this very virus. Unfortunately, we haven't been successful so far."

The group murmured in disappointment. Jason took a look around.

"Guys," he said, "Do you realize that this is the first relatively safe space that we've been in ever since this ordeal started?"

The others smiled and agreed.

"We'll have to head out tomorrow," said Captain Roger. "We don't know how long this space will be safe."

"I still can't believe the barracks were attacked," said Xavier. "Our men are *armed*. With the best artillery."

"Clearly, we don't know what we're dealing with here," said Morgan.

"I just feel bad for all the people in the barracks," said Zachary, "I wish we could have saved them."

Kate looked at him solemnly but then said, "We're doing all we can. We have to keep reminding ourselves of that."

The crew then turned in for the night. They gave Kate the sofa and the blanket. The rest of them huddled together on the floor.

Morgan and Jason settled down by the door. It was cool and dark outside. The stars glinted above them. They sat there in silence for a few hours. It was broken by Morgan when he saw a bat flying in the air. It was darker than even the night. He wondered how that was even possible.

"Isn't it strange," he said, "how the whole world changed all of a sudden?"

"Change is always sudden," said Jason, "But it's usually always for good."

"What good could possibly come of this?" asked Morgan.

"We don't know yet," he said, "But we can try to make it as good as we can. The only thing that we can do is do our best with what we have. See, the apocalypse brought us together. We are all actually a really great team: we watch out for each other and aren't trading people's lives to save ourselves."

"That's true," said Morgan.

'What's true?" asked Zachary. He settled down cross-legged beside them.

"What are you doing here?" asked Morgan.

"Couldn't sleep?" asked Jason.

"No, it's time for the two of you to sleep," said Xavier, joining the group and sitting cross-legged, too. "Zachary and I will keep watch for the rest of the night."

"But—" said Morgan.

"No buts," said Zachary, "You need to rest so that you can function tomorrow."

"Have either of you had any sleep?" asked Jason.

"Yes," replied Zachary and Xavier in unison.

So, the other two left and joined the huddle on the floor by the sofa.

***

The next morning, the group set out on foot again. The sun was hot and directly above them, but refreshed by a night of relatively better rest and safety than they'd had before, the group was in excellent spirits and had revived hopes.

They didn't know where they would go and how they would make it, but they knew that they would be perfectly fine as long as they stuck together.

Their refreshment buoyed a vibrant spirit, and the group marched across deserted planes in the heart of the mountains, cracking jokes and uplifting each other.

They were faced with a literal apocalypse. It was the worst thing that could ever possibly happen, and they knew not the way forward. The only thing they could do was manage their response and make it the best they possibly could. They refused to be defeated by this turmoil.

Perhaps it was for this reason that help came along. They didn't meet a single soul this far up and above in the mountains, but they didn't encounter any wild animals either. And, just as the sun was beginning to dim, Jason exclaimed with glee.

The others saw it, too. A highway stretched across the horizon towards which they were headed. And – the absolute best of all – an abandoned black Mustang was glinting in the corner.

The group raced towards it. Zachary hauled the duffel, which he had previously been dragging, over his shoulder. He broke into a jog. The sprint against the wind blew his hair back and flushed fresh air into his lungs.

They had been walking all day. Here, finally, was the reward.

Chapter 11: Morgan

The group faced a quandary: due to the elements of uncertainty either way, they couldn't decide whether to head up north or down south. Up north were the mountains; these were relatively safer, considering that they would reduce their chances of coming across zombies insofar as the group was aware. But while the remoteness facilitated safety, it also posed the danger of cutting off essential resources. Captain Rogers and Xavier were certain that they would eventually find a petrol station where they could stock up from the convenience store but admitted that they couldn't state the same for the presence of a gas supply. The authorities might have shut down the pipelines in an effort to preserve resources, which could leave them stranded.

On the other hand, heading south into the city would give them access to gasoline and other essentials, but at the expense of definite exposure to zombies.

"Let's take stock of what we currently have," suggested Zachary, "and evaluate how long we can survive with it."

"It's only two duffels," said Jason, unzipping the bag he was carrying, "How long could they possibly last?"

Morgan bent down on the ground and unzipped the other bag. The others helped him unload everything on the ground. They collected everything from the duffels and counted the items. After having chugged down most of the water due to the heat of the past two days, they concluded that their supply was insufficient.

“I should have grabbed a purifier from the mall,” said Kate, shaking her head in disappointment, “essential survival equipment!”

“It’s alright, Kate,” said Captain Rogers, “You just grabbed what you could at the time.”

“So, what do we do now?” asked Morgan.

“Well, it’s going to be dark soon,” replied Captain Morgan, “And we can’t sleep out in the open. We’re just going to have to set up camp somewhere.”

“We can go to the city, restock, and then move upward into the mountains,” said Zachary.

It seemed like a decent enough plan. In any case, it was the best that they could come up with at the time.

So, the group got into the car. Considering that there were eight of them, it was a miracle that everyone fit. But they were extremely cramped.

Beyond the windows – from which nobody except Captain Rogers, Xavier, Zachary, and Jason could see – all they could see was mountainous terrain.

The journey downhill was steady and smooth, but the sun was beginning to glow an orange rather than the bright golden it had previously been.

Still, there was neither a gas pump nor a convenience store in sight. As Xavier's eyes scanned the surroundings, he nervously gripped the steering wheel. From his place in the passenger seat, Captain Rogers looked for sign boards. He was trying to garner clues about their location so they could strategize where they could set up camp for the night. He glanced quickly behind him and spotted everyone squashed in their seats. There was no chance of them spending the night in the car.

Everyone in the backseat patiently endured the lack of space. They didn't even have room to squirm and were as silent as they were still.

They could tell that hours were rolling by as the sun descended in tandem with the vehicle. But the fading light intimated no promise of any place to stay. Xavier once switched on the radio, but it was completely silent. There was no static; it was just blank.

Xavier thought it would have been funny if a newsperson or radio jockey had gone to work during an apocalypse. *It would have been funny, but maybe we'd have found a way to communicate with them. And then maybe we could have reached them or at least figured out where we are*, Xavier thought bitterly to himself.

Xavier suddenly gasped. “Look!” he exclaimed, pointing his finger to a place beyond the window.

An onlooker would have, at this point, seen a stylish black Mustang pull over to the side of the road and into a gas station. The meter showed that the vessel was half-full, but Xavier decided to refuel it anyway. *Better safe than sorry*, he thought.

As soon as he parked the car, Morgan and Zachary immediately opened the doors. They stepped outside and breathed sighs of relief at the chance to stretch their legs finally.

Another car was parked right beside theirs, and it had Jason in it. Everyone was shocked and confused for a bit, as Jason was nowhere to be seen for the most part. He explained that he had to look for supplies on his own.

Later on, the others followed them immediately. Kate opened the boot and hauled the duffels out. She wanted to restock them at the convenience store.

But when she stepped up to it, the door was locked. Kate debated over whether to shoot it down but decided against it; there were better things to use ammunition for. It was only then that she realized how limiting of a weapon a gun was; it was functional only as long as there were bullets.

Then she remembered the hammer and struck it down hard on the lock. It gave way, and Kate stepped inside, along with Jason. The convenience store had already been ransacked. Every single shelf had been wiped clean, spare a film of dust. It had been empty for a while.

Dejected, Kate walked out of the store to see that dusk was settling in. The group was standing beside the car. They were trying to decide what to do.

So far, they had encountered neither the living nor the undead all day. This could mean absolutely anything and pose a huge risk. Without any news from the world, any strategy that the group came up with would be weak.

They were all beginning to feel anxious.

"The store's been ransacked," Kate announced. She dragged the duffels behind her, "but I don't understand how. It was locked from the outside."

"The store owners probably stocked up everything for themselves and their families," said Jason.

Zachary nodded. "In times like these, everyone's only looking out for themselves and a select few people alongside them. The world is more divided now than ever."

***

The car slid along the smooth road, the sound of its engine and tires the only one for miles around. The sun had set completely at this point, and everyone was feeling angsty and nervous.

Even this much peace could be eerie.

Everyone was lost in thoughts, each as racy as the others'. Only Captain Rogers was attempting to keep a cool mind. He was breathing in deeply: inhale four counts, hold for three, exhale for four again.

Suddenly, the car came to an abrupt halt. Jerked out of their respective reveries, everyone strained to catch a glimpse of what Xavier was looking at.

It was a large building on the side of the road. And, from the looks of it, the building was empty; no lights were on. There was no indicator as to what this place was except a signboard on the distant edge of the building's paved driveway. But it was invisible in the dark.

Slowly, tentatively, Captain Rogers opened the passenger door and got out of the car. He walked to the signboard while everyone inside held their breaths. Xavier pulled out his Smith & Wesson and unlatched the safety.

But Captain Rogers walked back to the group. As he approached, he gestured for them to get out of the car. Everyone did. As soon as they got out, the group pulled out their weapons. They proceeded toward the building, where the captain was now headed.

As they neared the signboard, they saw why the captain had gestured to them.

“Arnold Palmer Children’s Hospital,” Jason breathed.

“Are you sure this is safe?” Jason asked the captain.

“It’s the best we can do for now,” the captain responded, but even he seemed nervous. “Stay armed and close together at all times.”

The group surveyed the entrance of the building. A faded LED light was casting a white glow over the large white walls. The perimeter of the ground floor was covered with plants. Ahead of them was a set of escalators that led to the first floor. The whole place smelled faintly of antiseptic.

The group made their way up the staircase in front of them, walking due to the absence of power. Zachary thought it was good that they could smell antiseptic rather than rotting flesh; the latter would have indicated the presence of the undead-

Jason screamed. A hoarse groan behind him was quickly overridden by a louder, more painful scream.

Morgan had been bitten. A decaying creature was clinging to his arm with its teeth. From this distance, Zachary could not tell whether it was a male or a female. Zachary froze from the shock of it. He had heard no shuffling sounds. He had smelled no rotten eggs.

Both Jason and Morgan were attempting to shake the zombie loose, but the creature would not let go. Its teeth pierced through Morgan's flesh, and the site of the wound was beginning to drip.

Drops of blood splashed onto the white marble tiles below.

Everyone on the stairs suddenly recovered from the shock and rushed down to help free Morgan. Xavier shot the creature from a distance.

It remained unperturbed from the pierces in its thighs, shins, and stomach and continued to grip Morgan's arm, chewing harder now.

Morgan's face was beginning to turn grey. A horrible expression of agony was locked into his face. The pain was enough to kill him. He could feel his muscles tearing underneath this creature's surprisingly sharp teeth and ridiculously strong grip. The creature smelled of antiseptic. From this up close, it did little to mask the putrid stench underneath, but Morgan could feel that the creature had slathered it on like perfume.

These creatures were too intelligent. Morgan began to prepare for his death. Suddenly, he felt a swoosh of air from the tip of his shoulder down to his forearm. And the grip on his arm loosened. The zombie's head collapsed onto the ground, as did the rest of its body.

Kate stood before him, holding a katana with both hands.

"Where did you get that?" Jason asked her, eyes wide.

"Upstairs," she said, "You guys might want to head up there and take a look."

So, the others followed her up the staircase. Morgan pressed a piece of cloth to his wound. He closed his eyes in fervent prayer, wishing he had not been infected. Jason and Zachary gripped him from either side.

He heard a low gasp and opened his eyes. A carnage had happened here.

The dead bodies of zombies and people alike scattered the floor. There was, however, one interesting thing to note. The bodies of several people were clad in warrior outfits, particularly the white robes typical of Samurais.

"They came here to help us..." Captain Rogers said, his voice holding a mix of disbelief and amazement.

The world had collapsed completely, and divides had been cleaved – divides that prevented collaboration but rather the whole world in competition for survival. And yet, in the middle of it all, a group of warriors had traveled to this part of the world to help them. They had lost their lives in an effort to do so.

Morgan looked from the sight before him back to his own wound. His palm was wet. The rag that he was covering with – which Jason had handed to him – was thoroughly seeped.

As Zachary and Jason stepped forward to examine the carnage, looking for clues, Morgan's vision began to darken.

He felt a horrible wave of nausea and immediately sat down on the floor. A cold sweat was breaking out on his body.

Before the others could notice, he had collapsed to the ground.

The thud from that motion was what made everyone turn around.

Zachary shot glances left and right. He spotted a stretcher in the corridor beyond the place where the bodies lay in crumpled crowds. He dashed toward it. Xavier followed.

They pulled the stretcher toward Morgan, now crowded around by everyone.

Captain Rogers, Jason, and Jason hauled Morgan onto the stretcher.

"We need to get him to an ER *now*!" exclaimed Jason.

But they would have to find it first. The group raced the stretcher down the corridor, banging doors on either side open as they ran. They were regular hospital rooms. They spotted a ramp at the end of the corridor and pulled the stretcher up it. It took them to the first floor.

It revealed, irritatingly, an identical corridor.

"There it is!" exclaimed Jason, pointing toward a door that was labeled 'E.R.' in a glowing red neon sign above it.

Without wasting a breath, the group hurled the stretcher toward it.

Chapter 12: Survival & Sacrifice

Everyone had been put in a terrible situation. Stress engulfed the group as they made their way to the ER. Amid the chaos, Morgan complained about how his body felt like it was being eaten alive. He was shivering; his face turned cold and pale, and his eyes teared up due to his excessive pain from the flesh wound.

While everyone tried their best to stay sane, Kate was not having it.

It was becoming increasingly difficult for her to see her friend in so much agony, which destroyed her mentally. On the way to the ER, she had dropped the katana due to the fear of her friend becoming the living undead. But unbeknownst to her, it had been picked up by Jason.

Zachary pushed the door to the ER, which appeared to be locked for some reason. It was an eerie sight since the building was infested with nothing but zombies. So, it indicated to most of them that there was, in fact, someone else in the building with them.

"Darn! the door won't open!" Zachary's attempts at opening the door were getting louder and louder.

He was kicking on it now, trying his best to get the door to budge as Morgan's face turned paler by the second.

"Please, please be okay. Just hang in there!" Kate exclaimed as she grabbed Morgan's hand. But it was quickly pulled away by Xavier, who felt extra cautious about this situation.

"Give me the hammer!" he exclaimed, looking at Kate.

Kate froze, unable to utter a single word; she couldn't come to terms with the fact that her friend was slowly decaying in front of her. It significantly impacted her; she was shivering, sobbing, and begging for someone to make him better, even when she knew it was impossible.

Pissed at her, Xavier pushed his hand into Kate's duffel bag and grabbed hold of the hammer, which he then used to bash on the door knob. After three failed attempts, the door blasted open, and they made their way inside, dragging the stretcher to the bed nearby.

To their surprise, a man in a white robe and a stethoscope was hiding under a table. It was clear he had thought the dead were here to finally get him. Zachary pulled Kate's katana from Jason's hand and ordered the man to get up so they could examine him.

"Arms! Legs! Neck! Right fucking now!" He screamed at the man as the rest of the team began to look around for enough supplies to slow down Morgan's gushing wounds' effects. However, they found nothing; the room was empty, and they were out of everything.

As the man in white was being examined, Jason barricaded the door just for safety by placing large objects in front of it.

"What the fuck are you doing?!" Zachary shouted at Jason, thinking this idea was stupid. "Where the hell do you think we will go if Morgan turns, huh?"

"He won't turn."

Infuriated, Kate responded to him whilst giving him a cold shoulder. Roger held onto the wounded Morgan and put him on the bed as they ordered the man in white to come and examine their friend.

"Check for his wounds, look into it, do something!"

However, he said he would agree on one condition: if Morgan were tied to the bed, it would be much safer for everybody since he was a threat now.

His wound was constantly bleeding, his hands and body slowly turning all shades of blue and purple as nausea tuned his stomach. It was like his wound was keeping track of his senses and diminishing them one by one, as he could not even swallow water anymore.

After they had tied him to the bed, his body started twitching. They could hear his heartbeat now, much louder and faster. Cold sweat beads began to form on his skin as he appeared to be in a state of limbo. He uttered nothing, but he didn't have to because his body said everything he was feeling. Unable to withstand the grueling pain, he closed his eyes and, with one deep breath, passed out.

Kate's cries got even louder as she saw her friend battling for his life before her eyes. She felt helpless and was lashing out at everyone. But when that didn't help, she eventually sat down, holding onto the passed-out Morgan's arm, sobbing uncontrollably.

She had been trying to keep her composure for the longest time, but she could not any longer. Kate started blaming herself for not being careful enough to let this happen, thinking this was her fault since it was part of her responsibility to keep tabs on her friends and comrades.

Roger couldn't take it any longer. He walked up to her and sat down with her, hugging her so she could calm down.

"I know you think it is your fault, but trust me, you don't have to blame yourself for this," his tone was soft, ensuring he let Kate let out all her emotions, only so she could pick herself back and feel better.

"It's all my fault. I was supposed to be there for him!"

"It's not. You tried your best to be there for him. This situation is very fucked up. We're just ..."

While they were speaking, the doctor was done examining the passed-out Morgan. He finally gave his verdict, announcing that Morgan was beyond saving. The wound had made it impossible for him to recover in any way. Through his examination, he showed them the veins popping out of Morgan's arms and neck and his skin that had slowly started decaying.

Without hesitation, Xavier mounted Morgan and pointed his shotgun at him. Jason and Roger quickly made their way to him, latching onto Xavier as they pulled him away from Morgan.

"What the fuck are you doing, Xavier? Have you lost it?" Roger shouted, grabbing hold of Xavier's collar.

Xavier fled from their restraints and growled at both of them as he pointed at Morgan.

"Look at him! He'll turn into the living dead!"

"Calm down. Let's figure something out."

"What is there to figure out, Roger?"

Xavier interrupted and tried to calm down the situation, but he did not want to listen to reason.

His concern was valid; they were involved in saving a person on the brink of death, and they would only get out of this situation safely if they were lucky. Morgan was about to turn into a creature only driven to kill, consume, eat, and convert a healthy human into a monster.

Without question, Kate pulled out her pistol, which she had stashed in her duffel bag, and aimed it at Xavier. She did not want anyone hurting her friend.

"I will not hesitate to pull the trigger, so back the fuck off!" she exclaimed angrily as the rest of them looked on.

Her frustration was also valid; it was her friend they were aiming to kill. Roger also pulled out the katana to avert the imposing threat. They were in a rut that involved being pitted against each other.

"Let's all talk about this," Zachary tried to diffuse the situation, but nobody was ready to listen.

He knew deep down that Xavier was right; Morgan was now a liability. Not only was he injured and on the brink of death, but he was also bitten by the same creatures that were driven just to kill and consume. But with little humanity left in his heart, he wanted to keep the situation sane enough to decide a proper outcome for the opposing group.

Roger insisted on finding a solution; they were in the ER, and they had a doctor alongside them, but due to the severity of the situation, none of them wished to listen to reason. Xavier wanted him dead because there was nothing else they could do, at least according to the doctor's assessment. Jason had no say in it because it was a life-and-death situation.

An all-out quarrel broke out. Xavier wanted Morgan dead so he did not pose a threat to anyone later, which was really smart of him in a situation like this. He was removing all superficial thoughts and deciding the safest outcome for the whole group. However, Roger and Kate stood firm and defended their friend. Zachary ultimately tried reasoning with Kate, telling her how Morgan being killed off would ensure their survival, to which Kate became even more incensed.

"How can you say that? He's our friend. We can't just do that. We can't. I won't allow it. There has to be another way."

"We have a doctor in the room, for fuck's sake," she added as tears poured down her face. She was not ready to let go of her dying friend.

Jason was aware of the pain Kate was feeling for her friend, but he was also aware of the dangers he might bring. He was also willing to help her in this situation, but he knew that helping her would end up worse. Deep down, he also knew Xavier was right about all of this, but he chose neither side; he stayed neutral and let their fight consume the room. He sat down next to the terrified doctor and asked him if there was a way to save their friend, but the doctor only frowned, letting his head drop in silence. This made it very clear that it was indeed the only way to deal with Morgan.

They needed to kill him and end his suffering.

The arguments reached such a crescendo that they both started mounting pressure on each other. Both of their ideologies crashed into each other, and all of their emotions spiraled, filling up the room with enough noise to alert the undead.

The zombies slowly marched the hallways now, unbeknownst to the people in the room. As their conversation and violent motives grew, a loud thud was heard on the door. It was a lurker on all fours, marching in the room through all the blockage. It spewed blood and saliva from its mouth as it crept slowly toward them. Everyone with a weapon aimed and fired at the lurking creature, but it was swift enough to jump on the doctor and bite his neck.

Before anyone could react, the lurker ran outside the room, dragging the doctor with him. The doctor's screams echoed through the corridor as the bullets failed on this one. Everyone was shocked by this sudden attack. But most importantly, they were worried about how they had wasted their ammunition. None of them could believe the kind of undead they had experienced.

It was an unusual event; usually, the dead feasted on whatever excited their tastebuds, and they kept doing it until they were done with it and then feasted on other victims. But this felt like a targeted attack. It seemed like the lurker knew who it wanted to harm and who it wanted to evade. It was very uncanny and unrealistic, considering what they had just witnessed.

"Well, the day just got better," Jason's sarcastic approach as he spoke to himself was quickly cut short as he swiftly barricaded the door all over again. This time, he made sure it was completely covered and well-maintained.

This act infuriated Xavier even more.

"This is exactly why I want him dead!" he screamed in frustration, pointing his shotgun at Morgan's head again.

But Roger subdued him, grabbing hold of him as both of them started fighting. Roger dropped him down with a knuckle to his gut, immobilizing him for a while as he held onto the shotgun. Kate rushed aim at the charging Zachary, who came to help his fellow. It was pretty evident that nobody wished for this unsettling argument, but they were forced into it because of the situation they had been led into.

As they were quarreling, a faint groan was heard from the bed. Everyone tilted their heads to examine, and to their surprise, it was Morgan. His eyes poured blood now, his wound had worsened, and his body looked like it had decayed completely. He was unable to move due to the restraints, but it was visible how desperately he wanted to be let loose. Kate rushed from the lot to come close to him, but he informed her not to.

It was grueling for her to even see him like this, so out of life, she broke down in tears all over again.

"Hey, why so sad?" Morgan spoke with what little strength he had left.

"We can't let you go this way. There has to be so-" Kate began, but he interrupted her before she could finish her sentence.

"There's nothing we can do. I can't bear this pain anymore."

He coughed, spewing blood all over himself, growing sicker by the second. He beckoned to be put out of his misery as his words slurred.

With one last breath left in his lungs, he whispered, "I cannot be just like them. Just kill me."

Chapter 13: One Kill Brings Two

Everyone tilted their heads, trying to comprehend what was happening, as they saw their dying friend injured and hissing. His wounds had swollen, and pus immediately filled them. His eyes became pale and red, and he began to look inhumane. His nervous system had kept him okay for the longest time, but it seemed as if it had also given up on him.

"Hey, don't make that face," he mumbled under his breath, looking at all of them.

Even his eyes had begun bleeding, and his body started twitching. Xavier started mounting pressure on the group again as he took Kate's gun.

"Kill him before he breaks loose and starts feeding on you fools."

An all-out war broke out in the room as everyone began punching and kicking each other. Jason was the only one trying to pull everyone apart from each other as the dying Morgan was left staring at all of them. Roger pulled the gun away from Xavier and tossed it aside as the fighting ensued. Roger punched Xavier's gut, immobilizing him temporarily.

"Motherfucker!"

"Keep that mouth, and I'll stomp on it."

Roger aimed the gun at him as he was stoic now, devoid of feelings for Xavier despite what they had gone through. It became clear that this situation affected him just as much as Kate. Still, he chose to keep his cool because he did not want things to escalate any further, which was obviously futile, considering the fighting they had to go through.

As their quarrel ended, Roger looked over his shoulder to notice that Morgan had passed away. His pulse was gone, and so was his heavy breathing. Foam kept spewing out of his mouth, and it indicated that he, in fact, was gone.

Upon seeing that, Roger closed his eyes and sighed, pulling Xavier up, who pulled himself free.

"Keep your shit to yourself, Roger."

Roger decided to march toward Morgan and point the gun directly at his head, looking at Kate as he closed his eyes.

"Cover your ears."

And as he said that, he pulled the trigger.

What followed immediately after the loud blast was silence, running amok in the room. There was now a hole in Morgan's forehead, one that gushed out blood faster than a waterfall, and as soon as the blood came out, it was of a darker shade of red, maroon to be exact. At the sight, Kate instantly began screaming; her temperament began to crumble as she marched out the backdoor of the room, which was less barricaded. She was unarmed and had nothing in her hands to protect herself. Her fit of mixed emotions enabled her body to move on its own because she could not stand the sight of her friend getting shot.

Roger lowered the gun and rested himself down on the side, sighing in pain as tears eventually trickled down his eyes. The only words he mumbled were,

"It has been an incredible honor, my brother."

Xavier was left astonished; he did not know if Roger was going to be this cold about killing his own friend. He had no words to explain what had just happened.

"Hey, Roger..."

"You saw what I did to him, right?"

"He was my friend," Roger added as he gulped a lump in his throat but asserted dominance the next second as he further added, "It took me a second to put him out of his misery. Imagine how much it will take me for you."

"Yeah, whatever," Xavier shrugged it off, but he was evidently terrified. He could not share his emotions, and rightfully so.

Another moment of silence crept into the walls of the room; the ER felt like a library. The only audible sound was the crickets that managed to chirp in the distant tree that was situated right next to the window. After a while of Kate's disappearance, everyone became a bit concerned.

"Hey, is anyone going to check on Kate?" Jason inquired as he shuffled through her bag.

"Did she not carry anything with her?" Roger asked as he looked around for her katana since her pistol was with him.

"No. What the fuck?"

"We should go check on her," Roger got up, startled by this exchange.

He pulled her bag behind his back and tightened his grip around the katana, stashing the pistol on his lap.

And in the fit of the moment, they heard a loud scream.

"What the actual fuck?" Xavier shouted as he got up with his shotgun.

Zachary got up as well, confused about what was to unfold.

"Guys, tell me that wasn't Kate."

Zachary exclaimed in terror, knowing that two of their teammates and a random stranger were devoured and killed right before them. They could not afford any more losses, but what they were about to experience would soon cause everyone to lose their sanity, especially Roger.

Without a second thought, Roger decided to march outside the room, dashing into the hallway to check who it was, and the rest followed him.

"Hey, asshole! Wait the fuck up!"

Xavier shouted as they ran into the hallways.

The shouting turned thunderous as it began echoing everywhere in the building, and Roger kept running. Xavier managed to come close to him as he was not listening to anyone.

Zachary, however, tripped in the nearby hallway by a zombie attempting to grab hold of his leg. He managed to kick his face away with consistent kicking, but the zombie was persistent.

"HELP!"

He screamed, alerting Jason to come back and kick the head of the zombie away, eventually putting a bullet in his head to put him out of his misery.

"Are you bit?"

Zachary checked himself like a maniac, hysterical, hoping nothing would show up. Since the encounter was very close, he did not want that to be true, and when he found out he was safe, they both managed to catch up to both Xavier and Roger, eventually getting stuck contemplating whether or not they should pass the dark hallway that stood firm against them.

Roger pulled out a flare from his bag and motioned it in front of the dark alley, full of the undead, lurking, crawling, and attracted by the light.

"Well, fuck."

Jason sighed as he reloaded his revolver, and Zachary held his pistol in his hand.

"If we manage-"

Xavier was interrupted by Roger, who unsheathed his katana back in his bag and grabbed onto the pistol while holding the light and shooting down all of the zombies in his path, one by one. Not even the zombies could stop his fit of rage and anxiety as Xavier joined in, cocking his shotgun and marching alongside him, followed by both Zachary and Jason, who aided their pursuit of the noise.

Roger began screaming as he rushed further, and the noise began getting lower, diminishing after a few seconds. He slowly began to lose his sanity and all hope of finding Kate, but that did not stop him from pushing through; he kept dragging all three of them until they ended up in an empty room.

It consisted of two broken beds, chopped from the middle as if something sharp had pierced it. There was blood everywhere in the room. Jason sat down and looked around as he gave it a whiff.

"This is fresh blood," he said, looking at the three.

They were all fearing the worst and did not want to believe that this blood belonged to Kate. Their assumptions began spiraling down as they started looking around to find more clues as to where Kate actually went.

Xavier cocked his shotgun again, moving forward as he gave the two signals to proceed to the right of the room while the others proceeded to the left.

Unbeknownst to them, there was someone, no, some "thing" watching over their every step.

Xavier took Zachary with him, and they both proceeded cautiously, trying their best to scoop up the mess and find the girl, while the other two, Jason and Roger, began searching for the undead in the room. They searched for a hefty 20 minutes, scrapping every corner of the room, trying to figure out where she could actually be. They couldn't go downstairs since it was infested with the undead, but they searched all the other rooms. Actually, all of them entered the hospital from the back door, which was parallel to the front door, and from there, they took the back stairs leading to the same compartment of the first, second, and third floors.

Three of them looked around and gave up after 30 minutes since they couldn't risk their safety anymore, but Roger was adamant that they keep searching.

"Hey, look, I get it, okay, we can't risk our safety," Xavier said as he gripped Roger's hand, which he instantly waded off.

"Roger, I know how you feel, but for once, I agree with Xavier," Jason added as he looked at him.

And as soon as they had spoken, they were visited by a limp hand that fell from the roof. It was chewed on and terribly ripped off of someone's chest. All four of them stared at the hand, slowly moving their head to notice a zombie stuck to the ceiling, with a fatally wounded Kate swinging beside it. The zombie had her neck gripped by his mouth. Her eyes were wide open, her body lifeless as her head was badly chewed off. It was half open, and the brain nodes were visible from the wound.

The zombie looked like a spider, and it leaped down on the floor on all fours, with the dead body of Kate in its mouth, which it was feeding off. It kept devouring the skin and eating every bit of her flesh and did not care if someone else was in the room, even though it knew people surrounded it.

"So, who's going to pull their gun out first?" Jason asked, too hesitant to even look at this monstrosity.

It was a really different zombie, the same kind that they had seen drag the doctor away from the ER. It seemed to leap like a frog, and its mouth could open wider than most undead, which was why it could carry Kate like that.

"Roger, don't!"

Zachary warned him, as Roger had nothing but anger and hate on his face for this cretin. He rushed in, swinging his katana toward the undead, but the zombie leaped off, jumped onto the wall, and continued eating the leftovers of Kate's corpse.

"What the fuck did I tell you?"

Xavier pulled out his shotgun and shot at it, which it seemed to dodge as well, now attempting to jump toward Jason. But he was tackled away by Roger, too furious and clearly the physically strongest amongst all four. He stabbed the zombie in the gut and shot three bullets down its mouth, which popped his entire head open. Xavier followed up to him and pushed him aside as he shot the undead thrice in the stomach, and the other two marched their way and shot its limbs just in case it decided to do something else that was vexing.

They were able to subdue the threat and eventually ended up stuck in a brief moment of silence that crept into the room. Since the gunshots had been very loud, they attracted the distant snarling, alerting everyone. Xavier dragged Jason and Zachary, traumatized and shocked for a minute by the threat they had to deal with, but Roger stayed in the room.

"Roger? Let's go, man."

Jason inquired as he pulled him from his shoulder, but he was still, stale even. His face showed no emotion as his eyes dropped. His arms and legs felt cold as he was watching over the corpse of his deceased friend, Kate. Her face had split open in two, half of her brains were splattered in the room, she was missing a hand and was brutally wounded in the abdominal region.

Zachary marched his way into the gate toward the hallway they had made their way from, but the snarling got louder, indicating that it was, in fact, this dark hallway that would serve as a path for the hoard that was about to approach them.

"Hey, we can't use this path. You hear the snarling and growling, right?"

Zachary inquired as he looked at his gun and asked Xavier to do so as well.

"Fuck, I'm out of ammo," Xavier added as he looked at Jason.

"Don't look at me. I'm saving these shells."

"Roger, how many bullets do you have?"

Roger still did not answer, completely out of his senses. It was like he, too, was a walking corpse. He didn't utter a single word, nor did he feel any emotion; all his heart had was resentment and guilt of his friends passing away, which was more than enough to break him mentally. Xavier approached Roger and slapped him in an attempt to bring him back to reality.

"Hey, asshole! Wake the fuck up! If you don't do something right now, all of us will be victims of this shit as well."

"I get it. I really do. I lost my parents the same way you lost your friends, but right now, we cannot grieve. We need to move."

Xavier added as he held onto his shoulder, to which he nodded after sighing softly.

"Let's go. We need to find a different way out."

The door in front of them was a no-no, so they opted for the door on the left, which was properly barricaded by wooden planks and nails. Zachary wanted to shoot the planks off, but Jason wanted all four of them to keep the remaining ammunition in case something else happened. So, using Roger's katana, they sliced through the door and made their way into the room that led to a staircase, taking them back to the ER from a back entrance. Zachary and Jason fled first, and then Xavier made his way, but as soon as Roger began to walk away, he heard a loud snarl, most definitely from right behind him.

He could not muster the courage to look back at the monster, so he just took his gun out and shot the zombie down with his hand placed behind him. It eventually diminished the snarling, and with one final look, he saw that it was, in fact, an infested Kate, who had been turned into the living dead. His heart broke even more, knowing that he had to witness the death of his friend again, and that too by his hands.

After a deep sigh, he looked down.

"It was an honor to serve alongside both of you. Rest easy."

Roger uttered these words as he made his way to the staircase and back into the ER room, where he united with the remaining group.

Chapter 14: The Lab

Xavier, Jason, and Zachary had reached the ER and heard the loud bang of gunshots reverberating in the entire hospital. They looked behind them only to see that Roger wasn't there.

"Where did he go? He was right behind us!" exclaimed Xavier.

They turned around and bolted toward the door just when Roger appeared, covered in blood and guts, holding an empty gun in his hand. He looked at the rest of them, and his desolation and despondency evoked pity and shock in the others. Without uttering a single word, Roger dropped the gun on the floor and walked past them as if they were not there. He needed time to process the gruesome death of his friends and the fact that he had had to kill one of them as a zombie.

"What did you do? Your gunshots made so much noise that they will attract the undead herd! I know you're sad about your little friends, but you have to get over it now!" yelled Xavier.

Roger stopped in his tracks and stood still upon hearing Xavier's insensitive remarks about his loss. He turned around and, grinding his teeth, sprinted toward Xavier with his clenched fist in the air. As soon as he punched

Xavier in the face, he cupped his eye and fell to the ground. It had all happened in such a flurry that Zachary and Jason were left with no time to react or stop him; they both stood there, witnessing the chaos before them.

"You motherfucker!" Xavier shouted at Roger as he covered his throbbing eye.

"Fuck, that's gonna leave a blackeye. I'm gonna beat your ass," said Xavier as he stood up and advanced toward Roger, who was seething with anger and ridden with grief.

Zachary and Jason stepped in to stop Xavier and tried to cool the already tense situation.

"He's grieving. He just had two of his friends die within twenty-four hours of each other. Your blackeye will heal in a few days, but his wounds – they'll stay with him for life," said Zachary.

"Yeah, man, just give it a rest. We've all had enough for one day," added Jason.

Huffing and puffing, Xavier walked away as he gave Roger a threatening glare that implied, 'This isn't over.' Roger stood his ground, loosening his tightened fists. Zachary and Jason understood the gravity of the situation and attempted to console Roger, trying to prevent another fight from breaking out. At this point, all they had was each other; they were each other's only hope now that their group had shrunk considerably in size.

"Guys! Now is not the time to go at each other's throats. We have to be united toward one common goal: to get out of here alive!" yelled Jason.

"Xavier, we know you have an ice pack for a heart. But the least you could do is feign empathy, even though we now possess none of it," he continued.

Xavier sneered at Jason and quietly dragged his feet to the other side of the ER, where he sat down on the floor.

Witnessing the mayhem before them, Jason and Zachary sat down near Roger in an attempt to comfort Roger.

"Hey, man, I know what you've been through. I'm sure it's no less than hell, but a good trick to help you feel better is to remember Morgan and Kate the way they were, you know," said Zachary. "And I don't just mean when they were alive, but before the breakout. Like back in the army."

Jason nodded, and Roger intently stared at Zachary and heeded his deep insight. The atmosphere was filled with loss and sadness, and a cloud of memories and nostalgia was cast over the dimly lit ER as the undead sprawled outside those confines. The snarls and growls of the undead echoed in the room and added to the hopelessness of the situation that the four survivors had found themselves in.

The three spent most of the night talking about the outbreak and their losses. Roger talked about his time in the army with Morgan and Kate. As a seasoned veteran, he had been through things most would shudder at the thought of; he bore the scars, both physical and emotional, of war with him, but the battle he faced right now was an inconceivable one.

He reached within his shirt from the collar and took out his dog tags, engraved with two words: "Platoon Six." He clutched it tightly around his neck and fiddled with it as Zachary, Jason, and Xavier listened to his heroic tales of combat and his unbreakable bonds with Kate and Morgan, which now seemed to have withered away in the wind.

"It was the year 2003. Kate, Morgan, and I were stationed in Iraq. Platoon Six." Roger said as the lights of the ER flickered above them.

"I remember how we used to sit around a campfire, kinda like how we're sitting right now. Back then, in the thick of war, we thought we were invincible..."

As he recounted his tales to everyone in the room, Roger's face was flooded with memories, and his voice grew somber. His eyes welled up with tears, which was an odd sight to witness, given that he was the epitome of both physical and mental strength. He quickly wiped away the emerging tear to stop it from streaming down his face.

"We were stationed for all of three years. We ate together, fought together, and returned home in victory. We beat the odds; Kate and Morgan survived the war only to be mutilated by flesh-eating zombies," Roger said, shaking his head as his voice quivered.

"I killed her... those gunshots you all heard... Kate became one of... them. I had to kill her."

Zachary and Jason remained silent; Xavier, on the other side of the room, was still fuming with anger but also tuned into the conversation that was taking place. His expression changed as he was filled with shock after Roger's confession. Even though Xavier had put on this tough façade of being brave and indifferent to the sufferings of his group, he was terrified on the inside. But he did not and would not express his fear or remorse because he felt such emotions made a man weak.

All their eyes and ears were fixed on Roger, holding within them understanding and a sense of empathy. As Roger fell into despair, his voice trailed into silence, and so did the room. It was a poignant silence as if they were paying tribute to the fallen comrades, who had fought tooth and nail for survival but eventually succumbed to the deadly virus. Roger vowed to honor the memory of Kate and Morgan, how he would continue to fight and stay alive for them, and that he would find a way to rid the world of the deadly outbreak.

Midway through his pledge, Roger had fallen asleep, and Xavier followed him soon after.

The only ones left awake were the two scientists, Jason and Zachary. Zachary, concerned about the growing tensions in the group, had a storm brewing inside him; something was bothering him deep inside after witnessing Kate and Morgan's death. He thought seeing the plethora of gruesome deaths would desensitize him, and eventually, his shock would cease. In reality, he was probably most affected by the deaths of Kate and Morgan after Roger.

He experienced a pang of overwhelming guilt; he felt he could be doing more for the world rather than cowering in this room. This recurring thought irked him until he decided to make Jason aware of his worries.

As Jason was about to doze off, he was pulled away by Zachary into the corner of the ER.

"Jason!" Zachary whispered, and he grabbed him by the arm and dragged him. "Listen to me!"

"Ouch!" replied Jason, as he flicked his arm to get Zachary to release it. "What's the matter? Did the zombies get in?" he said frantically.

"What? No! Jason, I need your full attention here," continued Zachary. "I've had just about enough of this – we need to find a solution. I'm at my wit's end, trapped in this rat hole with all the bickering and fighting! I have no plans to end up as zombie chow like Morgan or Kate."

"Alright then, tell me your plan, your grand scheme to get us the hell out of here! Because the way I see it, we're at the mercy of those two lunatics out there who would want nothing better than to tear each other to shreds!" responded Jason, whispering so that the others would not awaken.

"We need to think of a way to get out...to reverse this virus, somehow... and we need to think of one fast," said Zachary. "It won't be long before the zombies sniff us out and devour us. We can't hide in here forever, and we'll need their help."

"You're right. We're like sitting ducks. Those two out there, they're made for battle. You and I... all we need is a petri dish, a beaker, and a lab coat," Jason said. "God, I miss the lab. We spent all our time there, saving the world from deadly diseases. We were like superheroes. Except, instead of capes, we wore lab coats. If only we had our lab here, maybe we could stand a chance..."

The two shared a brief chuckle when Zachary suddenly paused for a moment; he looked at Jason, and his eyes twinkled as if he had just had an epiphany.

"What did you say?" asked Zachary.

"About what?" asked Jason, puzzled.

"The part about the lab coats and the beaker."

"Yeah, and... what about it?" asked Jason.

"Oh, my God! You're a goddamn scientist, for Pete's sake, Jason!" Zachary yelled in frustration. "Okay, what I'm about to say is totally crazy and might sound outlandish, but what if we *did* have our lab right here?"

"Right, where?" asked Jason.

"Here! At the hospital. This hospital, the one we're in right now, this is a teaching and research institute too, right?" asked Zachary, but his tone was laced with assurance as he already knew the answer.

Although their meeting was clandestine, their murmuring had resonated throughout the ER, and while Xavier was knocked out cold, Roger had woken up to see the two doctors missing. His first instinct was that they had met the same fate as Morgan and Kate, and he immediately stood up to find them. But when he heard them muttering amongst themselves, he followed their voices. He tiptoed across the room and, upon seeing them, hid behind the reception desk of the ER and quietly tuned in to their conversation.

Jason and Zachary continued their discussion to escape from the ER and reverse the zombie virus.

"If it's a research and teaching hospital, that must mean... there's a lab here!" Jason said loudly, his eyes widening, and the tone of his voice grew optimistic. He immediately lowered his voice and began whispering.

"God, Zachary! If we could just get access to the lab, we could devise a way to finally find a cure!"

"I know! All the damage that this disease has caused... we could bring some peace back to the world, and things would be normal again."

Roger's eyebrows raised, still hunched over the desk, baffled by the daring plan that was being devised, which sounded too good to be true. He thought about the death of his friends and was reminded that even before going to Iraq, he was not afraid of death; now was not the time to cower. It was the time to fight back, even if that meant venturing out into the unknown. Roger stood up and went up to Jason and Zachary to give his two cents on the matter.

The two turned their necks, and as they saw him approaching, Zachary said, "Roger... you're up. We were just..." the two looked at each other, hoping the other would give him an answer as to their covert plotting.

"I heard you two. Despite your best attempt at this 'secret' meeting, your squabbling echoed throughout this tiny-ass room!" said Roger. "Now, tell me: are you two *really* planning to save the world or something?"

"We thought we'd at least try. Zachary and I were heroes back in the day. We were making ground-breaking discoveries and cures for fatal diseases. We can't sit this one out. It's our moral responsibility," said Jason.

"And we need your help," added Zachary. "We can't do this by ourselves."

Roger stared at the mad scientists for a moment and, with a stern expression, said, "If you had told me even a year ago that I would be stuck in an abandoned and infested hospital with two doctors and one psychopath plotting to save the world from the zombie apocalypse, I would have laughed in your face. But, if there's even a tiny chance that we could do any good, I'll sure as hell take it."

Zachary and Jason threw their arms up in the air as if they had just secured a victory and looked at one another, cheering quietly. They were potentially going to save the world, but Zachary and Jason could not deny that they were equally as excited to get to work in a lab again, something they had longed to do ever since the outbreak. They had decided that they would, one way or another, find a way to get to the lab. The real question, however, was the *how.* As far as they knew, the ER was the only safe room, and all other parts of the hospital were swarming with the undead.

Amidst the whispers of Zachary, Jason, and Roger, Xavier had finally awakened from his slumber. He woke to find them huddled in a corner, and it seemed as if they were having quite a serious and intense discussion. He raised his eyebrows and strolled over to the trio to get wind of what they could be discussing. Xavier immediately became suspicious and interrupted them:

"What's going on here? Plotting to kill me and throw my body to the ravenous zombies outside?"

"As much as we would enjoy the sight of you being torn apart limb from limb by those zombies, we actually need you if our plan is going to work," said Roger as he looked at Xavier with contempt.

With a cocky smirk, Xavier said, "Oh, you need me now? Well, please let me know how I may be of service to you, gentlemen. I'm all ears," he said as he looked at Zachary, Jason, and Roger.

"Xavier, be serious for a moment and listen up. There is a state-of-the-art research lab within this very hospital. Zachary and I need to get there so that we can figure out a cure," Jason chimed in.

"Sounds simple enough," Xavier said sarcastically.

"Oh, it's far from simple... the trouble is, we don't know how to get there," added Zachary.

"The hallways are infested. There's no way we can make it out alive if we go from the direct route," said Roger.

The group then weighed out all the limited options at their disposal. They were barricaded in, and each of them knew that this mission to reach the lab safely was one that could be their last. But despite their differences, they knew they only had each other to rely on, and even though it was a long shot, they had to work together for the sake of the world.

As the crack of dawn approached, the group was still wide awake, thinking of possible ways to sneak past the horde of zombies and make their way into the lab without getting bit. They sat together and tossed around ideas, the best of which came from the most unexpected person in the room.

After a long silence, Xavier screamed abruptly, startling the others.

"How about the fire escape? We can climb the fire escape outside and get in through the window! It's fool proof!"

"The fire escape... that's genius!" exclaimed Jason.

"We need to work fast. We can't stay in this room much longer. The fire escape is our best bet!" said Roger.

"Today, we rest. Tomorrow, we move," said Zachary. "You bastards better save us all, or I'm going to feed you to the zombies myself."

The shroud of grief covering the entire room was now a cloak of optimism and dedication; all four of them were determined to save the world from this horrendous nightmare, even if it meant they would die trying. As the sun's rays radiated through the small hole in the barricaded window, they promised a new day of hope, possibilities, and a fresh start.

Chapter 15: The Power Surge

As the new day approached, the team prepared themselves to venture out in search of the research lab. They had concocted a bullet-proof plan to reach it, which would be a task and a half, given that it was in the opposite wing of the hospital, next to the classroom building. To do that, they would've had to walk a few kilometers across the parking lot and evade the horde of the undead at the same time. But in order to get out of the main hospital building, they had to create a diversion to clear their path, as the corridors were infested with the undead.

Xavier, Roger, Zachary, and Jason all gathered the necessary supplies for their exit strategy.

"Alright, everybody. Huddle up," said Jason. "We have some ammunition left, so use it wisely. Two shotguns with about half a barrel of bullets each and one pistol with a full cartridge. Oh, and one katana. The last thing we need is to fall short on ammo, so I suggest we scour the hospital for anything we can fashion as a weapon," he added.

"Jason's right. It's best to assemble supplies for defense like medical tools or medicine," said Zachary. "Now, before we head out, maybe we should go over the plan. Roger, would you do the honors?"

"You got it," nodded Roger in agreement.

“Okay. So, first things first, we need to get the hell out of the emergency room. The exit is two floors beneath us, but as we last saw, the corridors are swarming with zombies. That means we have to go through the fire escape to the floor below us. Then, we need to create a diversion to clear our path in the corridors to eventually reach the emergency exit door. Then we climb down the stairs and exit the building,” said Roger with great focus.

“We’ve been over this a million times. Enough talking. Let’s just leave! I’m dying to slash some zombie brains,” interrupted Xavier.

“Thanks for the helpful input, Xavier. Anyway, as I was saying, after we exit this building, we have to make it across the parking lot in dead silence and without being noticed. Simple enough?” asked Roger as he looked at the other three team members.

“And then... we reach the lab, where we will rid the world of this heinous abomination of a disease,” Zachary said in a low-pitched tone.

“Easy there, tiger. First, we need to reach the lab in one piece. And I doubt you and the other Einstein over there will get much far since you can’t even properly shoot a gun,” said Xavier, condescendingly, pointing to Jason.

“We will have you know that we have been practicing our aim, thanks to Roger here, the army man himself. And since the zombie virus outbreak, we've learned to defend ourselves," interjected Jason.

"Nobody likes a smart-ass, Xavier," said Roger. "Remember one thing: stealth is *key*."

The four packed their supplies, cocked their guns, and mustered every ounce of courage they could find within themselves. Being the toughest of them all, Roger removed the makeshift barricade on their window to gain access to the fire escape. He tried unlocking the latch on the window, but before he could open it, he quietly paused for a moment. The team, in their curiosity, gathered around Roger. They peered through the dusty window, and their expressions changed in an instant. They got to see something they had not seen since they were trapped: the ruins of the world. Abandoned buildings and cars, blood spilled on the streets and roads, not a person in sight; it was all so empty and silent. The once hustling and bustling city had been reduced to a giant graveyard, adding a sense of hopelessness to the already tense situation in which the four had found themselves.

"It all looks so... hollow. Like nothing was ever there," said Zachary somberly.

"We need to leave. It's almost noon. Gear up," said Roger sternly as he opened the window and threw his backpack on his back. He led the way, and the rest of them followed suit, descending to the fire escape one by one.

They tread lightly as if they were treading on ice. They had to be cautious and not attract any attention with the slightest noise. Roger was the first to climb down to the fire escape of the first floor, peeping inside through the window to scan the hospital cafeteria.

He signaled to the rest of the team that the inside was all clear and that it was safe for them to come down. They carefully lowered themselves down the stairs and joined Roger.

"Seems like the coast is clear. No zombies in sight," whispered Roger to the rest.

He quietly opened the window, which, by a stroke of luck, was unlocked. He mounted it and ducked down to fit himself through it. Soon, they all had successfully reached the hospital cafeteria, which was an easy feat considering the set of increasingly difficult challenges that lay before them. They walked to the doors of the cafeteria, carefully covering their backs and each other's. Roger opened the door to peer outside and was careful not to make a creaking sound. Roger had feared the worst and met his expectations: the corridor was packed with zombies. The rotting smell of flesh and the growling sounds escaping the zombies' mouths caused Roger to shut the doors immediately.

Roger turned to his team and, in a faint whisper, said, "It's swarming with them. We can't go in."

He looked at Xavier and told him, “It’s your time to shine.”

Xavier grinned as he was about to set in motion a diversion to clear their path. He walked back to the window onto the fire escape as the others prepared to dash through the doors to the emergency exit at the corner of the hallway.

“Good luck. And don’t die,” said Zachary.

“Save the luck for yourself. I won’t be needing it,” replied Xavier.

And so, he went on his one-man mission to create a distraction while the rest of them waited. Roger, Jason, and Zachary waited for the signal from Xavier to open the door, which could arrive at any moment. After a fleeting moment of silence, a loud bang was heard from the next room, which sounded like a gunshot. The plan was for one of the team members to sneak into the room next door and make a loud noise that would divert the zombie herd there. Then, the person would, once again, escape through the fire escape to the neighboring room and slip past the herd to join the rest. Xavier had volunteered to be the scapegoat, much in accordance with his daring and rebellious nature.

“That’s our cue! Run to the emergency exit, now!” yelled Roger.

The three sprinted to the double doors that flung open with great force, then slammed them in an inaudible bang, drowned by the growls of the zombies who all flocked to the room. They saw the flickering, neon-red exit sign to their left and ran at the speed of light. Roger stretched out his muscular arm to grab the steel handle and locked his gaze on the corridor to be wary of any threat. Jason and Zachary, whose pace was slower than Roger's, barely made it through the door but reached it in time. They drew large breaths and knelt on their knees in exasperation.

Roger looked through the small window on the door in anticipation as he and the group waited for Xavier, just like it was originally planned.

"Where the hell is he? He's supposed to be here by now!" yelled Roger in frustration, but there was no sign of Xavier.

"Let's wait for him. He should be here any minute now," said Jason, whimpering now.

"Do you think *they* got to him"?" asked Zachary, giving Roger a concerned look.

"We can't stay here much longer. We have to go without him," added Roger.

"What? No! We can't leave anyone behind!" yelled Zachary.

“We have to. Come on!”

The three reluctantly left Xavier behind, with a heavy sense of guilt looming over them. As they tiptoed the stairs with their guns in their hands, they made their way downstairs, one man down. Aside from Xavier’s disappearance, fortune had been on their side; they had easily reached the parking lot. Under Roger’s vigilant gaze and agility, the duo of scientists had finally escaped the confines of the hospital and managed to do so without a scratch. The team breathed a sigh of relief, which was interrupted by what sounded like the clink and clang of metal. They aimed their gun in the direction from where they heard the sound, which seemed as if it was coming from behind the dumpster.

Roger, Jason, and Zachary, now alert and on their feet, inched closer with Roger’s finger on the trigger. Their hearts pounded in anticipation as they perceived a threat approaching them, the heavy stomp of dragging footsteps growing louder and louder.

“It’s me. Don’t shoot, for fuck’s sake!” said a familiar voice from behind the dumpster.

The next second, Xavier emerged in front of them. He had managed to evade the herd of zombies alive and unscathed.

The other three gazed at him in amazement, lowering their weapons.

“You’re alive? How?” asked Zachary.

“A magician never reveals his secrets. Now, make haste. We’re only halfway through.”

“Wait,” said Roger sternly. “How do we know you haven’t been bitten?”

They all looked at him with suspicion.

“Ugh! I haven’t. See, no blood anywhere,” he said, doing a 360-degree turn to show them his untorn clothes.

Roger paused momentarily and, without uttering a word, walked over to the parking lot to get to the lab while the rest followed.

The zombies in the parking lot were sparse, so the team managed to avoid any encounter with the undead, keeping a watchful eye and hiding behind cars until they scurried over to finally reach what the team had deemed the promised land: the research lab. Up until this point, all four had succeeded in reaching the lab despite coming face to face with danger and had emerged from the claws of death. Their good fortune, they would soon realize, was short-lived as matters would start to deteriorate from here on out.

“We made it... I can’t believe it! We finally made it out of that dingy ER, and now we can figure out a cure!” exclaimed Jason as Zachary patted him on the back.

Roger, warily, looked back at the parking lot and swung open the doors of the lab. They all darted inside to seek refuge, and Roger immediately locked the door, searching for the light switch.

"Alright, nerds. Go on and save the world," said Roger sarcastically.

"Guys, we have a problem. There's no power!" Jason said, his voice laced with concern.

"Without power, we can't do anything. We need to turn it on," said Zachary as Jason nodded his head in unison.

"Great! Just what we needed. Where will we find the damn power board?" asked Xavier.

"We need to split up. That way, it'll be easier to find," said Roger. "Zachary, come with me to the floor above, and Jason and Xavier, you guys head to the basement."

"You know what they say... as soon as the team splits up, things start to go awry," said Xavier, as he let out a slight chuckle.

"Jason, behind me. Don't get yourself killed, and more importantly, don't get me killed. See you two on the other side," he said, winking at Roger and Zachary.

The team then split into two, hoping to restore the power, oblivious to the chain of events that was about to ensue; their good fortune would soon dry.

Xavier and Jason, walking through the dark corridors of the lab with nothing but a flashlight, ventured toward the basement. As they made their way down, they could not help but feel a sense of foreboding. There was an eerie feeling that Jason could simply not shake off, the creaking of the basement stairs invoking a sense of fright in him. They stumbled upon a huge wooden door that did not seem like it belonged there.

“I think this is the primary power board. See all the wires connecting. They lead behind the door,” Xavier explained, pointing to the tangled wires.

Xavier stepped toward the door, but before he could open it, he was stopped by Jason.

“I don’t like the feeling of this place. Let’s turn back,” said Jason, fretting with panic.

“Oh, come on. I like a good challenge!” replied Xavier, consistent with his risk-taking nature.

“Let’s not be rash. I say we contact the others, and then we can decide,” Jason replied.

“Fine. I never get to have any fun!” Xavier pouted.

The two decided to retreat, not knowing what awaited them behind the basement door. It could be a trap or, worse, something malevolent hiding in the shadows.

As they retreated, their footsteps echoing through the empty halls, they spotted Zachary and Roger approaching them. The two were determined to open the door together to restore the power, unaware of the danger beyond the door. Xavier and Jason exchanged wary glances, silently conveying the gravity of the situation.

"We checked out the first floor, but Dr. Genius here speculated that the power board would most likely be in the basement. So, we thought we would mosey on over here and join you two," said Roger, who seemed rather hopeful.

"Why haven't you guys opened the door yet? We need power," added Zachary.

"I don't think it would be wise to open that door. Who knows what's behind it? We made it safely all the way from the hospital building to the lab. I'm not about to die in a creepy basement," announced Jason.

Unbeknownst to them all, behind that very door lurked an unimaginable horror—a horde of zombies. Once renowned scientists who were trying to figure out a cure to the disease, much like Jason and Zachary, had now been turned into ravenous monsters. They were the ones locked away in the facility. Their lifeless eyes hungered for human flesh, and shuffling footsteps echoed eerily through the quiet halls.

The team had no idea what they were up against, and the tension was palpable. They had to be cautious, for their lives depended on it. Xavier and Jason quickly warned Zachary and Roger, sharing their concerns and the urgent need for caution.

Despite the peril, the group knew they couldn't turn back. Restoring the power was crucial, not just for their own safety, but perhaps for the fate of humanity itself. The stakes were high, and they had to press forward, facing the unknown with courage and determination. Everyone looked at the door for a moment, carefully calculating their next move.

“Guys, the whole building is empty. There are no signs of the undead anywhere. I’m sure the door has always been there. We need to open it,” said Roger. “Should anything go wrong, just be prepared to run.”

With their hearts pounding, the team decided to open the door for what lay ahead. The facility's secrets and dangers loomed large, and the zombies lurking in the shadows were only one of many challenges they would have to overcome.

In this abandoned facility, shrouded in darkness and uncertainty, the team's fate hung in the balance as they embarked on a perilous quest to restore the power and confront the undead horrors that awaited them.

Chapter 16: Evil Trapped

Their hearts were beating like a kick drum, fueled by an aggressive drummer. The rumbling each time it pumped blood, the anxiety, the tension, and the anticipation rose as all four of them slowly approached the basement. They knew they had no other route to reach the lab, which was the only way they could change the course of the peril that had enveloped this blue planet. Although all four of them were hesitant, Roger urged them to be headstrong and take on any challenge that lay dormant behind the door.

Exhaling, Roger stretched his arm toward the doorknob and slowly opened the door. The creaking noise it made filled the room with terror.

"Roger, wait!" Zachary yelled as he held onto Roger's hand.

"Hey, what gives?"

"Have you not watched any horror movies?" Zachary spoke adamantly.

The entire gang looked on in utter confusion.

"What the fuck?" Xavier whispered as he barged between Zachary and Roger, kicking the door open.

A long silence followed. Their eyes went numb to the sight they witnessed, and they stood frozen in place.

However, Xavier was unfazed since he was looking at his peers and not at the door he had just opened.

"What? Why is everyone so pale?" he said, angry at the lack of response.

"Speak the fuck up, dumbasses!" Xavier yelled as he heard a low hissing sound coming directly from the door.

Since the lights in the basement kept fluctuating, only a glimpse of the room could be seen at a moment's time. Xavier narrowed his eyes as he moved the beam of his flashlight so he could see better, only to be frozen in place as well. What he saw terrified him.

"Zach..." Roger whispered lowly.

"Y-Yeah...?"

"What about horror movies did you want to mention?" Roger said, looking at him as he unholstered his revolver from his lap.

"I think we just got a taste of that."

Zachary grabbed hold of Jason and began marching upstairs in a state of panic. Xavier followed the two as Roger closed the door behind them and started running. But since the door had already been weakened and barely held on to its hinges, it was blasted open. As soon as the door crumbled, they heard loud growls followed by even louder footsteps that seemed close behind them.

"Why didn't you spit this shit out before?!" Roger screamed at Zachary as they ran for their lives, trying to keep their ammunition in check as they did not want to waste it immediately.

"What the fuck do you want me to expect? I've never been here before!"

Zachary slipped one of the stairs and fell face-first onto the stairs, spraining his ankle. As he grabbed his leg, he heard loud thudding and hissing, instantly freezing in his place as he, too, thought he was in huge trouble. The images of Morgan and Kate started playing in his head almost instantly as he began hyperventilating. Xavier marched back downstairs to grip Zachary by the arm and placed him on his back, carrying him upstairs.

As they marched upstairs, the rumbling footsteps began to thud louder than before, and Xavier felt fatigued from all the carrying, ultimately slowing him down in the process. Feeling immense fear, Zachary looked back, only to feel his heart stop at the sight: a horde of the undead, making their way toward them, hellbent on the group's demise. They were not just regular zombies; these lurkers were dashing on all four feet, their faces disjointed as their lower jaws hung from the remaining flesh of their faces. All of them looked genetically modified, adapted to the strains of the virus that was spread in order to cause this outbreak.

Zachary began to scream.

“Asshole! Why are you screaming in my ear?!” Xavier slapped him on the leg, running with every ounce of might he had in his legs.

“Xavier! We’re gonna die! I’m so sorry, but we’re gonna die!” Zachary screamed as he began shivering.

“For fuck’s sake, you two!” Roger jumped in the action as he shot three lurkers down with his revolver. But he noticed that as soon as he shot them down, the four-legged freaks did not die. Instead, they got back up and began running even faster than before.

“What is this terminator shit?” Roger shouted as he helped carry Zachary back to the glass door that closed the basement from the compound that led to the lab.

“Guys! Hurry up!” Jason screamed as he held onto the door connecting the compound and the basement, waiting for the lot as he was also worried about the undead that followed. As soon as they reached the door, Xavier dragged Zachary to the lab, and Jason and Roger held onto the door while mounting blockage in front of it so that it would down the hurdling horde, giving them time to regroup in the lab.

“Okay, time to make a run for it!” Roger shouted as he joined the three in the lab and slid onto the floor as he slipped, but since the doors were locked the second they entered, they felt relieved. They saw that the compound now became the only place that separated them from the zombies, and they were just moments away from being devoured by the undead.

"Remind me to let you finish your fucking sentences, Zach!" Roger screamed in anger and confusion but stopped talking as he saw how traumatized he was.

Roger slowly approached the shivering mess and sat down with him, holding his shoulder as he rubbed it, reassuring him that they were away from danger for now. After a while, Zachary did calm down, and as his senses returned, he stood up to see the compound, which was now infested with the undead.

"Yup, we're trapped," Roger spoke from a distance.

"The zombies broke into the compound right after you passed out. The door to the basement is completely crushed; there's no way out of this hellhole either," Roger explained to him.

"What do you think we should do?" Zachary asked, looking at a concerned Roger.

"Honestly, I'm not sure. Our only exit was from here."

"Where's Xavier?" He looked around but could not find him, only for Roger to point at him.

"He's finding supplies and a way we could make a run from here."

A heavy sigh emitted from Zachary as he collapsed onto the side of the table in the lab, his head resting as he was tired. He had never experienced a near-death incident that shook him to the core. Realizing the immense danger they were all in tore his morale and confidence, making him so terrified that he felt like avoiding everything. He felt sorry for himself since he froze, but he did not share his deepest emotions with his peers. However, being observant, Roger sat down with him and rested his head back at the table.

"I know what you're feeling, Zachary. I've been there."

"I'm not sure how you've been there, but thank you for being here with me," he spoke softly, looking at Roger.

With that statement, the silence broke between the two, making Roger uncomfortable. He did not want to tell them what he felt, but he felt as if it was important to put out, considering the situation his comrade was in; he wanted him to feel better because that was how he was. He wanted them to feel somewhat consoled before they attempted to escape because he could not afford any more causalities. With one deep sigh, he spoke as he gulped a big lump of unease.

"... Before I pulled the trigger on Kate, I felt frozen... stuck in place. I couldn't think of anything."

"I just couldn't handle the fact that one of my comrades got infected and eventually met their doom, and I don't want that happening to you. I just can't," said Roger, a stream of slow tears becoming visible under his eyelids and onto his cheeks.

Zachary saw him as they both shared a hug, expressing their heartfelt hurt and pain. It was a defining moment between the two since both felt loss and emotional toil the most at the given time. After a few minutes, Zachary composed himself and nodded, indicating that he was okay, and so did Roger. As they both got up, they looked at Xavier, who entered the scene.

"The only way out here is by burning this lab."

Roger marched towards him and smiled sarcastically, then proceeded to add, "Xavier, what kind of drugs are you on?"

"I'm serious," he spoke, his tone stern.

"We're locked in the lab, though. What could go wrong here?" Jason added as he looked at the surroundings.

"That is if you rely too much on the glass we're enclosed in," Xavier pointed at the glass, made very weak from all the knocking and hurdling. There were visible cracks on most of the enclosing, which peaked Zachary's anxiety even more.

Roger looked at Zachary and instantly spoke, "But we're safe here, right? For how long do you think we can survive here?"

"Here's a bright idea, dumbfuck. Ask the fuckers lurking in the compound hellbent on chewing out our brains!" Xavier screamed at them, beginning to drag a barrel of chemicals toward the lot.

The tumbling and shifting caught the attention of the undead that lurked outside, who were now knocking on the glass doors of the lab. All of them got alerted as they began grabbing onto their weaponry, as panic took over them.

"Way to go, Xavier. You single-handedly sped up the whole demise act for us!" Jason spoke sarcastically, rolling his eyes as he gripped his gun.

"Hey, I had to, okay! Someone had to do something!" Xavier yelled as he gripped his gun.

"Okay, so who's going to take the Terminator zombie out?"

"The fucking what?" Zachary looked at Roger as he said that.

"The one that's on its four legs and for some fucking reason does not die?" Roger explained as he held on to his katana tightly.

"Can we please fucking focus? We cannot outrun them!" Xavier spoke as he kicked the barrel close to the door.

"Bro, what the fuck was that for?!" Jason screamed as he hid behind the table.

"That is very inflammable! Why would you do that?" Zachary took cover as well as they barrel rolled and hit the glass door, alerting more zombies. So now, the glass walls were full of zombies, clawing and striking to make their way inside.

"Xavier, what do we do?" Roger looked at Xavier as he held onto his katana even tighter, preparing to tackle the invasion.

"We need to blow this place up. There's no way we can survive." Xavier aimed at the barrel but was stopped by Roger, who shook his head, indicating that he had a plan.

"You take cover. As soon as they march in, I'll blow them up from the entrance. It might create an opening from where you guys can make your way out," he told Xavier, sheathing his katana and unholstering his revolver.

At first, Xavier was hesitant, but then he began looking for something amidst the messy lab, only to bring a heavy book that could act as a decoy, opening the door enough to expose the entire compound with the big can of chemicals placed at the gate.

"You wait for the signal. I'm going to throw this in the compound, and as soon as you see the rubble clear, you open the door, toss the can outside, and shoot, got it?" Xavier shouted as he looked at Roger, to which he nodded, watching as the zombies began to devour the gate.

Xavier began to march to another gate barricaded with wooden planks and slowly began opening it in a desperate attempt to protect his comrades. As soon as he did, there opened a shallow entrance through which he tossed the book. Thankfully, the book was enough to distract the lurkers, pushing them away as they drew them away from the lab. As soon as it did, he looked at Roger, giving him the queue to attempt his part of the deal. As soon as Roger opened the door and kicked the barrel into the compound, Xavier took cover.

"I'm so fucking tired of all of you," Roger spoke as he shot at the barrel of chemicals, which instantly caught flames.

The flames were so potent that they entered the lab as well, breaking into the glass doors and engulfing everything: the tables, the doors, the infrastructure, everything caught fire. The loud boom of the barrel pushed Roger back into the lab, and his head hit one of the tables, rendering him unconscious. And as for the undead, the entire compound was full of burning bodies of zombies screeching and crying in pain.

Their hissing became so loud that it reminded Zachary of the shouting and screaming Kate emitted during her demise. It made Zachary relieved to think that they had managed to avenge their fallen comrades. But amid the chaos, he now had a few problems of his own: an unconscious Roger and a severely wounded Xavier, who had gotten caught in flames. Similarly, Jason was stuck between the glass and broken debris of the tables, keeping him busy for the most part, too. The only person conscious enough to notice was Zachary, who was horrified and relieved by the screeching misery of the undead.

Chapter 17: Death & Ashes

As Zachary saw the compound engulfed in flames, his face's curvature changed, and a low grin spread over his face. He slowly started to enjoy the misery of the undead, and watching every single one of the cretins begin to cremate and crumble, he started shouting and screaming in joy.

"Serves you right, you fuckers! Die!"

As Jason rose from the rubble, he started looking for his gun, but he couldn't move since his leg had wooden debris stuck to his flesh.

"Fucking hell..." Jason whispered, limping around now.

Xavier slowly made it to Jason and held onto the broken wooden plank that had gone through his leg.

"Okay, don't scream," Xavier spoke as he held onto the plank.

"You think I'm a pus- FUCK!" Xavier removed the plank before Jason could even finish his sentence and saw him scream at the top of his lungs, but he placed his hand on his mouth and covered his leg with a piece of cloth he had ripped from his shirt.

"God, you really are a chick!" Xavier scoffed as he covered the leg nicely and helped him on his shoulder; they both now looked at Zachary, who suddenly went silent.

They saw his legs shake as he started vibrating in a split second. It was purely because of fear, and as they both slowly approached Zachary to check up on him, they stopped midway and held onto their weapons.

"Oh, not this again..." said Xavier, agitated as three zombies were on all fours in front of them. Their eyes glistened red, and their mouths opened in two different compartments, revealing their tongue, which was as long as Zachary's palm. They slowly marched towards Zachary as Xavier reloaded his gun in the nick of time, in case the bullets did not affect them as much.

"Oh great, it's the Terminator zombies again," Jason muttered under his breath and looked at Xavier, both aiming right at them. As soon as both reacted, one of the zombies leaped forward and grabbed Zachary, dragging him with its extended arms to pin him against the shards of glass. Meanwhile, the other zombie instantly jumped to grab Xavier but was instantly subdued by a gunshot to the brain, splattering the remains of its brain all over the floor. This alerted the other zombie, but it was taken down by Jason, who leaped to stab it in the head, followed by six more stabs just for safety measures.

"God, give me a fucking break! I just had a wooden shard down my leg."

As Jason finished taking care of the Terminator zombie, he looked upward, only to find another horde inviting danger toward the survivors. Xavier ran toward Jason and picked him up, instantly remembering Zachary's situation since he was busy before.

"ZACH!" he screamed as he proceeded to look back at his friend, who was about to become zombie dinner.

The sight was really disturbing; the zombie began licking Zachary's terrified pale face and kept snarling, intimidating him to the point where his voice box gave up. Cold sweats began slowly trickling down his spine as he knew for sure his demise was near. As the zombie's snarling grew even louder, Xavier bolted toward him, catching up to him as it opened its mouth to fulfill the promise. But suddenly, Roger tackled the zombie down and tossed it off the terrified lad. He ran toward it almost instantly and fit three rounds of lead down his cerebral, instantly killing it.

The sight of the zombie was one thing to be terrified of, but as soon as all three of them noticed Roger, they saw someone else. It was like the undead, only driven to end the lives of whatever harmed his comrades without any remorse.

"You three, get going," Roger spoke as he looked back at all three of them. Xavier ran to grab Zachary, who snapped back into his senses. He saw Xavier and Jason slowly limp toward him as the three regrouped to notice how Roger kept glaring at the cretin that was approaching their broken lab. But before Roger could do anything stupid, Xavier slowly gripped him, dragging him to the bunker behind the broken rubble.

"You dumb shit, don't even think about it!" Xavier shouted, but the undead heard it much clearer.

They started running towards Roger as he was being dragged away by Xavier. In the nick of time, Jason and Zachary made it to the bunker, awaiting Xavier and Roger. The bunker that they hid in was protected from the inside out in case of a fire or a bombing, so it was the best place to hide. But as soon as Xavier made it to the gate and started dragging Roger in, the undead bit into Roger's arm.

"FUCK! Get off!" Roger screeched as he started kicking the undead. Since the grip was too tight, he looked back at Xavier one last time and spoke,

"Close the door."

"What the fuck? No!" Xavier shouted, but as soon as he saw the situation they were in, his heart dropped.

"God fucking no... " Xavier mumbled incoherently as he saw that the undead was feasting on his arm. Roger struggled, punching Xavier to push him back and gripping the door handle to slam it shut.

"Son of a bitch..." Zachary mumbled as he saw the bunker close and slowly walked up to Xavier to help him up.

"Were you bit?" Jason asked Xavier as he started examining him but was dismissed.

"Does it fucking look like I have a big ass tongue?" Xavier growled as he looked at the closed bunker door, trying to figure out what had just happened.

"He's gone. He was bit," Xavier said while digesting a big lump of pain down his gullet.

"Oh no..." Jason whispered as he sat down and held his head.

Meanwhile, in the broken lab, Roger was being overpowered by the undead as it began pushing its teeth ever further down Roger's arm.

"You're one stingy bastard! GET OFF!" Roger shouted as he shot three rounds of his revolver that opened its head inside out, which released its grip as soon as its brain painted red on the entire floor. Roger tossed the zombie off in a fit of rage and unsheathed his katana, taunting the zombie with it.

"Fine then, if this is the end, I'm not going down alone."

The zombie suddenly leaped forward, and with one swing of his katana, its head hit the floor. Roger mocked more of them as they emerged from the fire, engulfed completely in debris and flames. Since Roger was already very pissed, he smirked and gripped his katana, bolting toward the undead this time.

As he did, a horde followed the enhanced zombies, but he managed to swing his katana and take off the heads of six. With every passing minute, he proceeded to kill as many as he could, with a total count of twenty zombies. But as he continued killing them, he started feeling nauseous. In a fit of curiosity, he looked down to notice his arm covered in blood. His veins had started turning black, indicating that he was, in fact, slowly succumbing to the virus. Within a few minutes, he was surrounded by six more zombies, which he easily evaded by swinging his katana.

"C'MON, YOU FUCKERS!" he shouted as he hit one knee, slowly turning paler and weaker as he scoffed at the marching horde.

"So, there were more of you, after all, you sneaky bastards," Roger said as he got up again and started chopping off more heads.

Now, as he began to kill more and more hordes, he saw his left arm completely give up; the life inside it diminished. He started limping as his body began to deteriorate. As he hit his knee again, he started breathing heavily, his eyes slowly losing focus. As his vision started to diminish, so did the strength in his legs. With every ounce of energy left in his body, he got up again, with the revolver in his hands now, shaking as he did not know where to look or shoot. He started examining the area as more zombies approached him, but this time, they managed to overpower him, pinning him against the floor as he was rendered helpless. They began chewing down his flesh, bit by bit, organ by organ, as he left a smile on his face and aimed directly at the unused chemical can nearby. It was his plan all along to take out the entire lab with him if they ever ended up in a situation where one of them eventually got bit.

As soon as he was about to shoot the container full of chemicals, Xavier entered the lab to help his comrade, but he was stopped immediately by Roger, who screamed with the last breath he had in his lungs,

"It has been an honor serving by your side!"

It gave Xavier a clear indication that he should run for his life, and without wasting a second, Xavier closed the bunker doors, dragged Zachary and Jason out of the bunker from a different exit, and dashed out of the building.

"What are you doing, Xavier? What about Roger?!" Jason screamed as they exited the building immediately.

They reached the exit and were significantly away from the building, but their footsteps were stopped by another modified zombie, who was killed immediately by an enraged Xavier. He shot the zombie with all the rounds of ammunition he had and started shouting in anger, but it was hindered by a loud explosion that was heard by the three survivors.

They could only watch as the entire laboratory came crumbling down. Jason instantly hit his knees as he saw their last hope of bringing peace to the world completely vanish in front of their eyes.

"That was... That was our last hope of survival..." Zachary muttered, his words slurring.

His body began to shake, and tears welled up in his eyes. He started laughing hysterically within a few seconds as the trauma finally caught up to him. He had seen so much death until now and so many incidents where he could've been killed. He thought of himself as a liability because he was nothing but a scientist... and that was it.

He was taken out of his trance as Xavier slapped him across the face, which made Jason enter the scene and grab hold of him.

"What the fuck did you just say? Last hope of survival?" Xavier asked as his face flashed red in complete and utter anger.

"Xavier, calm down," Jason whispered as he held onto him.

"Our survival was compromised since the day the fucking outbreak became a pain in our asses, but we still managed, did we not?"

"Both of you need to fucking gather yourself. We need to make it to find shelter," Xavier uttered as he broke loose of the restraints and gripped Zachary's collar.

"And if I find you crying like a bitch in front of me, I'll make sure I end your life before those fuckers even get a chance to snarl at you. Am I fucking clear?"

Zachary stared right into his eyes with fear and anxiety, unable to share any words.

Jason slowly marched toward Zachary and patted him on the shoulders, helping him up as they saw Xavier slowly walking away from the scene and reloading the gun he held in his hand.

"Let's go, Zach. We need to go," Jason spoke as he began walking.

With one last glance at the crumbled building, Zachary, too, joined the lot, slowly making their way into the vast unknown.

Hours passed, and all three of them kept walking, their heads bowed, prepared to either die or fend for themselves at any moment necessary. Zachary had to compose himself since he knew being paranoid in a situation like this led to nothing but catastrophe. They could not afford to make more noise and make their existence known because if they did, they were unsure what dangers lurked in the surroundings.

Moreover, their discovery of genetically modified zombies kept them scared and alert, so they had to be careful about how many bullets they could use. Xavier was only left with three rounds of ammunition, and Jason was left with none, so he resorted to his knife. Zachary kept the shotgun Xavier had given him, but he did not know that his gun had no shells left. Just two more for immediate use and discarded if they ever ran into something they wanted to dispose of instantly.

Their venturing slowly led them to a secluded forest with many dead bodies, presumably killed off before they set foot there.

"Stay on your guard, everyone."

Xavier spoke as he led the three into the forest, but they were stopped in their tracks by a zombie standing still but not facing them. Zachary was about to shoot it but was immediately stopped by Jason.

"Are you fucking dumb?"

Jason slowly approached the zombie and slit its throat from behind it, and kicked it away in an instant. He followed it with several stabs to the head, and once he was done, he pulled his knife out, cleaning it using its clothes.

"Stealth - don't make any noise."

And just like that, whenever they encountered another undead lurker, they would kill it silently just to avoid making any sound. Zachary almost tripped and got eaten alive, but he made sure to keep himself composed throughout their journey.

They sought refuge in the forest after a couple of hours of walking and ate the last of their supplies just so they could feel a bit refreshed.

But Zachary was still not feeling hopeful. Letting their situation get to his head, he broke down and began to scream at the top of his lungs, which alerted Jason.

"What the fuck? What's wrong?" Jason asked as he began to examine him to check if he had been bitten or something.

"They... They are all dead... What will we do...?" Zachary's words started slurring, and tears started streaming down his cheeks.

He was instantly put to silence by Xavier, who covered Zachary's mouth with his hand.

"What the fuck did I tell you about you making noise? You're going to get us killed!" Xavier screamed, slapping the screaming Zachary to shut him up.

But it did not work, as his fear had already consumed him completely. As he was shouting, Jason noticed emerging footsteps, which alerted Xavier as well, and both put their guards up almost instantly.

"Thanks for nothing, Zachary," Jason muttered, appearing agitated.

Xavier pulled out his gun and started looking around. As they began to inspect the nearby bushes, they soon found themselves surrounded by a horde of zombies that had arrived from the depths of the forest. Xavier turned to look at Jason, terrified beyond measure, and then back at the walking dead as they slowly marched toward all three of them.

Watching the situation they were in, Zachary started contemplating the choices he had made that led them here, the moments where he could have composed himself even more so than he did and wondered if he was the reason their survival was compromised.

As night fell around them, they had no choice but to brainstorm on how they were supposed to evade the imminent danger in front of them if they truly wanted to live.

Chapter 18: The Forest Rut

It was 7:45 p.m., and the night loomed over the three survivors as they slowly made their way further and further into the forest. Xavier was carrying Zachary on his shoulder, and Jason followed the two slowly. He was unable to follow them at their pace due to the invasion they had had to deal with before. Zachary had passed out due to the sheer trauma the invasion had brought him; he had never seen Jason this angry or vicious in his life, so much so that Xavier couldn't even go help him. He had single-handedly wiped off thirty zombies with just a combat knife and all the weapons in their possession, so it was evident that they were out of ammunition and out of options.

Jason was covered in the remnants of the undead, coated in blood, remains of their organs and flesh, and both Xavier and Zachary were too scared to ask him to take them off. His eyes went completely dim from all the exhaustion as he was low on sleep, but they insisted on walking until they found a safe spot to camp. Zachary had been unable to deal any damage to the undead as the sheer trauma the horde brought him had rendered him unconscious. Xavier couldn't do anything since his weapon was taken by Jason. His furious actions would have gotten all three of them killed, but he was in no position to listen. Xavier was still very confused about how Jason had managed to pull that off, but he was too focused on their safety for it to matter.

They trudged deeper and deeper into the pitch-black forest, and their attempts to find a safe spot felt futile now. Xavier knew that if they did not find a spot soon, they would eventually have to face death; there was no other option. But Jason remained optimistic; he knew there was hope in finding at least some place where they could seek refuge. But none of them spoke to each other about it, as Xavier was too scared to speak to a furious Jason.

Jason was always the comedic relief, being the sarcastic and the most sensible amongst the trio, and with Roger, he had blended well despite their differences. With Roger gone, Jason had reached a point of collapse and reacted like the undead. The blood lust for the lurking ghouls had become evident on his face.

Mustering up the courage to utter a word, Xavier asked Jason, "Are you okay?"

His tone was soft and careful since he did not want to invoke Jason's anger.

"Never been better," Jason spoke bitterly.

"I don't think there will be any place for safe refuge. We need to put up shelter here," Xavier spoke as he carefully held Zachary on his back.

"No can do."

Jason only spoke in one-sentence answers. He was in no mood to respond or explain himself, but Xavier persisted in asking for his opinion. He wanted to know if they were on the same page, which clearly wasn't the case. Jason wanted them to carry on with the plan to find a place for refuge, but due to exhaustion, Xavier was unable to. The fact that he was carrying Zachary also meant he was physically more fatigued than the rest of them.

"We need to stop, Jason, or we won't be able to make it anywhere at this rate," Xavier said as he stopped and looked at him. But Jason did not wait and kept walking.

"Where the fuck are you going? Jason?"

Jason suddenly turned around and punched his face, compromising Xavier's balance, who fell on Zachary, which also woke him up. The thud that followed was very loud and alerted the nearby undead again, which began running toward them.

"God, not again-"

Before Jason could finish his sentence, he was ambushed by a running zombie that got on top of him and began biting the air in front of him, hungry for flesh. But Jason managed to toss it off him, giving him enough time to draw his combat knife and slice open its neck. Jason saw as two more began to march toward Xavier and dashed to double-kick one of them, giving Xavier enough time to get up and aid Jason in the ambush.

"Left or right?" Jason asked, gripping his knife tightly, but Xavier kicked Jason instead and mounted on him in a rage.

"Can we do this after the murder machines are done devouring us?"

"Let's sit back and find out, asshat!"

Xavier threw a punch at him, which Jason easily deflected, and then threw his knife into the skull of one of the zombies, instantly killing it. He then proceeded to toss Xavier off him and rushed to grab his knife. Xavier landed at the feet of another zombie and punched it, which eventually caused the zombie to fall. He then proceeded to break the zombie's neck using his bare hands, which was risky, but he had to since they were out of bullets and melee weapons. He ran back to Jason and jumped on top to punch him, only to get hit by the handle of Jason's knife straight to his gut. He fell to the ground, clutching his stomach. While he was dealing with this, he saw another zombie was about to reach Zachary, but before he could reach him, the zombie's brain got painted all around the forest, following a loud noise emitted by a shotgun.

Jason instantly looked at the source of the shotgun bang he had just heard and noticed a woman wearing an all-black camo suit, which blended well with the forest bushes. She instantly bolted out of the scene as she saw her presence becoming well-known.

“HEY! YOU!” Jason screamed, beginning to follow her.

“HEY, ASSHOLE!” Xavier ran after him, picking up Zachary and carrying him on his back.

Jason began running faster than Xavier to catch up with the woman, but he eventually slowed down since the fatigue finally caught up to him. He kneeled right at the last second, enabling Xavier to catch up and kick Jason, causing him to fall on his face. Xavier quickly got on top of Jason and started punching him, fist after fist, as his anger got the best of him.

Zachary joined in to drag Xavier off him, but he punched Zachary away, mouthing, “I’ll kill you if you come closer.”

He then slowly continued his fist fury but immediately stopped as a gun was pointed at his head.

“Get off him right now! You murderer!”

Upon hearing those words, Xavier instantly looked up to find the same woman, dressed in black, aiming right at his face.

All the color vanished from his face.

“You land another hit, and I’ll paint the entire forest with your fucking blood!” she threatened him, cocking her shotgun.

“Yeah... you tell her...” Jason mumbled, having trouble breathing due to his bruised face.

"Who the fuck are you?" Xavier spoke as he looked at her angrily.

"I'm sure you don't remember me, assholes. You only know how to hold a trigger," she replied sternly.

"With all due respect, madam, you're doing the same," Jason mumbled as he coughed blood.

"Do you want your ass saved? Or do you want to join him?" she spoke, aiming the gun at Jason.

"Oh, no, no, I'm just being neutral about this. My apologies..." he said, closing his eyes and sighing in pain.

"What the fuck do you want?" Xavier spoke as his agitation peaked.

"You seriously don't remember, do you? I'm sure you remember the little girl you took from me: Emily," she spoke as a big lump caught up in her throat. She gulped and aimed the gun at Xavier again.

"Doesn't ring a bell."

Xavier responded, grabbed the gun, and tilted it to a side. The shotgun went off, barely missing Jason. Xavier attempted to grab the pocketknife in Jason's pocket to slice open her throat but was tackled immediately by Zachary, who entered the scene to stop him.

"ENOUGH!" Zachary screamed, anger clouding his actions.

He picked up the shotgun that had fallen because of the wrestling and aimed it both at Xavier and the woman.

"NO MORE! NO FUCKING MORE!" He screamed at the top of his lungs.

"Stop shouting, you asshats! You're going to bring more undead towards us..." Jason mumbled as his face went sore from all the punches he had endured. The screaming had alerted the nearby zombies, who slowly began crawling towards them. Amongst the crawlers was a Terminator zombie, as described by Roger.

"Knock yourself out for the fourth time..." Jason said, lying there with his eyes closed, awaiting death any second now as he was out of strength and ammunition.

Xavier saw the zombies and instantly leaped in to grab Jason's knife from his pocket.

"Yeah, go ahead, take everything from me, you bastard..." Jason said with one last breath and passed out.

Xavier proceeded to dash and slice open two of the zombie's necks but got into a wrestling match with the third one. Zachary passed the shotgun back to the woman, who took care of the Terminator zombie and shot it three times in the chest, but it still got up. By the time it did, she was out of shells.

"What the hell?" she looked astonished, unaware of the zombie she had just seen.

She had never seen something like this before, and it had startled her. Zachary wanted to help the latter two, but he got caught up in dealing with two zombies. He only had three rounds of bullets left in his pistol, which he had just found out about.

"Screw this!" he shot one of the zombies, missing him, as the bullet hit its ear, flinging off immediately. He fired once again, and it took down the zombie, unraveling its throat inside out, causing his head to fall off from his neck support.

Now that all hope was lost and everyone was out of all ammunition and options to fend for themselves, they started panicking. They all knew they were heavily outnumbered and outmatched, so they just silently accepted their defeat and waited for their collective demise.

"PATTERN UP, YOU LOT!"

A distant scream was heard from the forest, instantly getting their attention. Loud thudding was heard from within the deep woods as they heard screams and cries of zombies being decapitated and tossed away. They saw one of the zombie's bodies come flying into the scene, his torso being ripped into shreds by slashes from a melee weapon. The head of the zombie was so cut up that it became hard to identify who it was.

Suddenly, the loud thudding stopped, and silence crept into the vicinity, redirecting every lurker's attention toward the area where the screaming was heard. Suddenly, a man riding a horse jumped into the scene, holding a katana as it began slicing every single zombie's head in one false swoop. As the Terminator zombie instantly latched onto the horse's flesh with its teeth, the man jumped off the horse, landed on his feet after a barrel roll, and pulled his revolver to shoot the zombie down, filling its skull with three rounds of lead. Since it was bait, the horse ran into the vast distance, neighing in pain. But that did not concern the man as he made his way to examine the survivors, checking each one's pulse one by one and then pulling them up on their feet.

"Thank God, you're here!" the woman exclaimed as she hugged him.

"Anytime, love, eh?" he grinned as he diverted his attention to the three survivors, aiming the tip of his sword at all three of them.

"Say, will the bluds budge up?" he said, raising his eyebrow as his facial expression turned more serious.

"What the fuck did he just say?" Xavier spoke as he looked at the man speaking, unable to understand due to his accent.

"He asked if you guys were okay. Can you move?" the woman responded.

"Do you not see us on our feet?" Xavier answered.

"Isn't this wanker full of beans!" the man responded, slowly walking toward him, aiming his sword as he added, "Oi, listen up! I get the whole 'Macho Libre' act, but that ain't gon' change the fact that your arse got saved by me, so I suggest you keep the dilly dally to yourself, eh?"

The man grinned and tapped the tip of the sword on his cheek as he withdrew it.

"You're lucky I don't have a weapon right now, you asshole," Xavier responded, his anger peaking immediately. But that only excited the man, and he proceeded to look away from him and walk off.

"Since we had a good chinwag, let's be on our merry way now, Cheerio!" He started walking away, using a flashlight to illuminate his path.

"Hey, wait! Can we please come along with you?" Zachary responded as he called him out in an act of plea.

"And what on God's earth do you think I ate before I had to choose between that, you mutt?" he replied with a smirk.

It infuriated Xavier again, who moved forward with a clenched fist but immediately stopped as he aimed his revolver at him.

"Easy there, Bambi!" the man responded as he tilted his head with a glare and smirk, getting Xavier to stop immediately.

"Ugh..." Xavier mouthed as he looked at Zachary.

The man then aimed the gun at him and said, "You want in? Tag along. As for your unconscious friend, take him with you, but you, you're one big pain in the arse, you stay!"

He aimed the gun first at Zachary, then at Jason, and then at Xavier to explain who he wanted to tag along with him.

"Steve, can we just go?" the woman inquired as she held onto the man's hand and looked at him.

"We can't just leave them here, love," Steve answered, caressing her cheek and sighing as he gestured to bring the three along.

The night became even darker, and the only visible path was from the light emitted from the flashlight. Xavier carried Jason on his shoulders now since he was the only one physically capable enough to do so. Steve led the way along with the woman, seemingly cautious on the way to their destination.

"Where exactly are we going?" Zachary asked.

"To the bunker," Steve responded as he kept on looking for the path.

"What's that?" Xavier inquired skeptically.

"A gaff, four walls around a vast haven that encompass all the lot that survived this shit hole," Steve answered as he tilted his head to look at him.

"I swear to God, can someone translate this fucker for me?" Xavier asked, looking agitated, incapable of understanding the slang Steve had used.

"Steve was in the army, back in the United Kingdom. He was brought here on a mission that revolved around a mysterious outbreak where people were attacking each other, and he ended up being stuck here eventually," the woman answered.

"Why'd you ask Xavier if he knew you?" Zachary asked her, concerned about the company he was in.

"Do you remember Sarah Desmond, Xavier?" Steve asked as he stopped in the path and glared him down.

"I hooked up with a lot of women in the past, so be more specific. OF COURSE, I DON'T REMEMBER!" Xavier answered, snapping at him.

"Keep your tone down, arsehole. You'll wake up the wankers," he reprimanded him, keeping his tone calm and stern.

"You killed my daughter back when we both were in the shelter. I survived the outbreak that led to the mass destruction of the haven we were in before. My daughter was ill, and you just took her away from me mercilessly..." Sarah answered, gulping a big, painful lump down her throat but remained strong and gripped onto her shotgun tightly.

"With all due respect, were you sure she was bit or just ill?" Zachary asked.

"She was bit..." Xavier answered hesitantly after a brief pause.

Steve caught the hesitation.

"NO, SHE WASN'T! YOU LIAR!" Sarah shouted at him as she gripped his collar and pointed Steve's revolver to his chin, growling.

"So, nobody is going to tell her to shut up now?" Zachary asked sarcastically, looking at both dueling it out.

"Save it for the haven, you two. We're almost there," Steve called out as he lowered the gun from Xavier's chin.

Sarah sighed and followed Steve, and all of them did the same. After twenty minutes of walking, they came across a big metal gate covered by barbed wires and electric fences, completely guarded from the outside.

"Ah yes, home sweet home!" Steve snickered as the gates opened for him, and he invited all of them inside.

As they entered, their eyes shot open to the view: houses with electricity, children playing around, houses refurnished, slow music, and samba playing in the distant background. It was like a town come to life, and seeing that brought all of them joy. They were so happy to finally see a civilization that they started investigating it. Steve was very vigilant, however, keeping close tabs on the three of them.

"Welcome to the haven. Consider this your complete pitstop for a while," Steve said with a smile, showing all three of them their quarter to spend the rest of their night.

"Food, resources, anything, you let me know, all right?" he said, leaving the house but making sure he kept a guard outside to check on all three of them like a spy.

Xavier placed Jason in bed and went to clean up, washing his face and taking a shower. He sat down on the balcony but was approached by Zachary.

"Xavier."

He tilted his head to notice Zachary behind him. He gestured to ask him what he wanted.

"What was she talking about?"

Xavier stayed silent and did not answer the question.

"Was she right, Xavier?" Zachary further inquired.

“What did you do with the woman’s child?” Zachary insisted as he had an idea of what had happened. He just could not grasp the thought of what or where it all happened. All of them had done unthinkable things, but this one in particular kept Xavier on the edge of his seat.

The silence broke into the room, and flashbacks came, invading Xavier’s peace, and that got him speechless and sweating. However, he did not do or say anything; he just stayed silent and looked away from Zachary.

“Xavier, tell me honestly, what did you do?”

“Nothing,” Xavier replied as he held onto a matchbox, took a cigarette from his pocket, lit it up, and started smoking it.

“You better not get us into trouble,” Zachary warned, leaving the room and Xavier traumatized by his thoughts and actions.

He just sat there, limp and numb, knowing what he had done, as the screaming of a dying child came to haunt him. It made him drop his cigarette, giving him a panic attack that immobilized him.

Zachary noticed everything happening with Xavier, and it all made sense to him slowly. However, he decided to leave him alone for a while as the night finally concluded.

Chapter 19: The Revenge

As the sun rose the next day, Xavier's cigarette stayed dormant on the floor of the quarter. It had been lit but wasn't smoked, so it was clearly intact. But there was no sign of Xavier anywhere in the quarter, nor was Jason's. They were both missing, and the only person present was Zachary.

Zachary had woken up, not because he had had a good sleep, but from the sound of people shouting and screaming. And it wasn't just anyone screaming; he realized that it was the familiar voice of his comrade. So, he got up as fast as he could and made his way down his quarter. As he walked towards the echoing screams, he noticed Xavier and Jason pinned against the ground with guns aimed at their skulls.

He froze in place as he saw Xavier being beaten by batons while Steve stood there and just watched them. Zachary wanted to help but was unsure how to make a move. Contemplating a plan for a few minutes, he just flung himself into the scene and kicked one of the guards with the baton, ultimately getting captured and beaten as well.

"Say, can you Adam and Eve this? All the misfits banded together, mate!" Steve chuckled as he held onto the baton and jammed it right into Zachary's skull.

As soon as it hit him, he fell on the ground face first, unconscious, while everyone else was forced to watch.

Xavier was infuriated but couldn't do anything since he was restrained by handcuffs, courtesy of Sarah, who wanted revenge for all the damage he had caused her.

"Now I reckon it's a dive, but which one of you wankers will spill first?" Steve asked as he bent down to tower above the three and tapped Xavier's head with the baton, wanting quick answers.

"I told you; I know nothing!" Xavier screamed as he growled at Steve but eventually had a baton hit his face. It left a nasty bruise on his cheek. But it did not faze him since he spat the blood in his mouth at Steve right afterward, coating his face.

"You let me out these chains, and let's square up, just you and me asshole!" Xavier shouted again as his anger peaked.

But Steve did not acknowledge him; instead, he wiped his face with a napkin and put it back in his pockets as he ordered the guards to pick him up.

"Uncuff him, let's see how dishy he can be," Steve said, smirking, and watched him get uncuffed.

But as soon as he was rid of the handcuffs, Xavier charged at everyone like a wild animal, knocking both the guards out by taking their batons and using them against them. When he was done with them, he saw Steve standing wide open, waiting for him to attack. To put a cherry on top, he taunted Xavier, provoking him to attack. Xavier took the bait like the short-tempered mess he was.

As soon as he rushed, Steve moved to a side and kneed his gut down, immobilizing Xavier almost instantly. He dropped down to his knees and spat blood as Steve watched and laughed.

"C'mon, I thought you were more than just that," Steve mocked him as he kicked him in the gut again.

Xavier couldn't do anything but groan in pain while he was being pummeled repeatedly.

"THAT'S ENOUGH!" Jason yelled as he started crawling on the ground but was put down by another guard, who swung a pole to his wounded leg, making him scream.

Both men were just being used as punching bags now as Steve slowly broke every single part of Xavier one by one, from his ego to his anger. Then, finally making his way to his bones, he ensured Xavier was not allowed to commit another heinous act again. Eventually, Steve learned what Xavier had done from Sarah, but he kept it under wraps since he wanted to break the news when she was around. She was sent on a mission to collect tree bark and supplies for the survivors.

After a while, Sarah arrived on the scene atop a horse. She made her way to the compound of the haven, only to notice the three captives against large poles. Sarah dismounted and marched slowly towards the three, noticing Xavier finally waking up and looking at her dead in the eye.

"Top of the mornin' to ya, mates! Today, we are gathered here for an auspicious moment! The execution of three tyrants!" Steve spoke loudly as a crowd gathered to witness the moment. He wanted to make this scene very public because he was the boastful kind; he liked to express himself, and since he was the leader of the haven, people loved him for it.

Steve was a UK Marine Special Ops captain who had been sent on a mission to infiltrate a top-secret non-governmental organization that was responsible for the undead's widespread. He got stuck here after every single person in his squadron turned into the undead and devoured everyone in that building, leaving him the only person to survive. With the help of a few bandits he met along the way, he made the Haven, a bunker made solely to group together the finest of survivors and ensure the safety of mankind from the deadly fiends that ran amok. He made sure the Haven's defenses were as tight as a military base. Since he had all the knowledge he gained from the Marines and the experience on the battlefield, he made sure to implement them to preserve everyone enclosed in the four walls he helped mount.

Sarah stood there, not listening to what Steve had to say. She only yearned for Xavier's blood and death.

"You know what you did, Xavier," Sarah mouthed, scowling at him, but he did not respond. He merely continued to stare at her.

"Confess, goddamnit!" Sarah screamed again, making her way onto the ramp that led to the poles to which they were tied, only to be held back by Steve. Even he was finding it difficult to hold the woman together, whose anger came out in various waves and actions. She kept moving her arms, punching and kicking the air, and cussing at Xavier.

All he saw was a delusional and rage-driven woman.

"YOU FED HER TO THE UNDEAD! YOU FUCKING ASSHOLE!"

After she screamed that, a collective gasp was heard, and everyone in the crowd started growling and screaming in anger. Xavier knew it was true but did not want to confess just yet.

In the meantime, Zachary looked at him, saying slowly, "Is she the same girl...?"

A long pause stretched between the two, and Xavier gave him an affirming look, which traumatized Zachary. Jason was unaware of the situation, and he just looked confused. He did not know what to say or expect.

"What are they saying, Xavier?" Jason asked, looking at him. But it was futile since none of them spoke, and Jason only noticed how Zachary's face went pale, presumably from the horrors of what Sarah had spoken about. He turned to look at Xavier, who looked down, his expression cold and indifferent.

"What did you both do...?" Jason asked, looking at both.

"Oi, let the tall cretin go!" Steve spoke as he looked at Jason, pointing at him with his revolver.

He was immediately removed from the ropes, and the platform underneath him was hit.

"Do you have anything to say?" Steve inquired, aiming the revolver at Jason.

After a brief pause, Jason spoke.

"Hey, whatever happened in the past, I know for certain that Xavier wouldn't do that without any reason. In fact, nobody would do that without a reason! I'm sure there was a reason. You should at least listen to Xavier's side of the story before deciding to bash them completely!"

Steve raised an eyebrow and shot his revolver in the air, staring down at Jason now. He knew something was up between the three, but he still gave Xavier a chance to clear his side out.

"You heard your lad. Go on," Steve said, now aiming at Xavier.

Xavier looked at Steve and stayed silent. He knew it would risk their safety if he spoke up about what had happened. But he also knew the consequences if he did not speak up since Steve was in no mood to negotiate; he was here to act as judge, jury, and executioner.

"Go on, motherfucker!" Sarah screamed as she tossed a bottle of water at Xavier, but Steve stared her down.

He was agitated by the woman's tantrums and wanted to solve this, not create a scene since he had changed his mind.

"You do that one more time, and I'll have you tied up instead!" Steve shouted, aiming the revolver at Sarah now.

"You, wanker, speak the fuck up, I'm tired of y'all," he added, turning back to Xavier.

Silence stretched among the crowd as Xavier found it hard to clear his case. It was gut-wrenching how Emily had died, and the flashbacks came marching in. It got him shivering again, causing him to panic internally as he thought about every detail of the incident. Zachary watched him and realized he looked paler than before. He felt bad for his comrade but couldn't do anything. He then looked at Steve, who was looking at him as well. Steve noticed how pale they both looked and decided to aim the gun back at Jason.

"I'll give you sissies a countdown. If none of you speak up, one goes down," Steve spoke.

"What the fuck?" Jason looked at the two and then back at Steve, and before he could escape, the guards gripped his arms and held him in a lock, pinning him down on the floor.

“Choice is yours, Xavier,” Steve slowly walked towards Jason, held the gun close to the back of his head, and glared Xavier down, unlocking his revolver's safety.

Xavier, still nonchalant, did not care because he could not risk either of their safety.

“5.”

“Xavier, listen to me. We’re going to be okay. Please tell them,” Zachary spoke in a state of panic as he looked at him. He started tugging on the restraints, wanting to be set free.

“4.”

“Xavier?!” Jason screamed, tugging on the guards' grips, but was instantly struck by Steve on the back of the head with the revolver's handle.

“3.”

Xavier’s heart started pounding faster than before; the risk he couldn’t take was to sabotage their safety, but now Jason was in trouble, and so was Zachary. They were pinned, and the gun aimed right at Jason’s head further solidified that they were, in fact, in danger. He knew they would both lose their lives if he didn’t speak, but he couldn’t form words. He couldn’t bring his throat to emit any sort of noise.

"2."

"XAVIER?!" Zachary screamed at him as he began tugging more vigorously.

"FUCK YOU, SCREW THIS!" Jason screamed as he tried his best to escape the restraints.

"1..."

"WAIT!" Xavier finally screamed as he looked at Steve.

"Oh, for fuck's sake, I was about to have fun!" Steve screamed, still aiming the gun at Xavier. "What is it, bark!"

At that moment, Xavier felt speechless all over again. He was contemplating whether it was him trying to save his comrades or himself. But regardless, he mustered up the courage to speak.

"I- I fed the child to the undead," he spoke hesitantly, his head dropping down in shame.

Everyone in the crowd started shouting and approaching the platform where they hung, infuriated by his confession. They wanted justice for Sarah's daughter. However, Steve felt relieved that it was off Xavier's chest because deep down, he knew it had to be done. Sarah had told him everything about what had happened, so he knew why Xavier had to do what he did, but he wanted him to confess so that they could've been let out easily.

It was his plan all along.

Steve aimed the gun at every single person approaching and shot it in the air, scaring them. They stopped in their tracks.

"Before you fuckers decide to send this man to a kip, I suggest hearing the lad out," Steve spoke as he rubbed the nozzle of the gun on his temple, clearly showing his agitation in small gestures, and sighed. He looked at Xavier next and gave him a reaffirming look so he could speak up and clear his name.

Xavier looked at him and exhaled loudly, then looked at them as he spoke.

"I did it; I fed the child to the undead, not because there were any personal grudges. We were held at the bunker, and Sarah and her child were gravely infected. Her entire arm was infected with the same virus that changes us into living monsters. I left the child to die and be fed on because I could either let the monsters devour me and all the people in that bunker, or I could've used someone already dead as bait to lure them away for our safety. That child was already a living zombie! There was nothing else I could've done."

"YOU PATHETIC LIAR! YOU TOOK EVERYTHING AWAY FROM ME!" Sarah shouted, infuriated.

She began charging towards him but was contained by Steve as he aimed the gun at her.

"Can you fuckers, like, shut the fuck up?" Steve shouted, now looking at her.

Everyone went silent in an instant.

"You guys want justice? Fucking fine. I banish you three! You three better leave this shithole by morning!" Steve shouted as he asked the guards to let go of their restraints, and they did.

"And now, till they are here, if I see anyone even dare march to their quarters, I'll have their heads."

Steve dismissed the case and told everyone to scram. He was so agitated that he did not even bother looking at the people responsible for all this rut. He just let them off to their quarters.

"WHEN THE FUCK WILL I BE OFFERED MY GRUB?" Steve shouted as he began marching to his quarter, stretching as he swung his gun back in its holster.

"This is not what we promised," Sarah gripped onto his arm, stopping him in his tracks as she growled.

"Lady, you heard what he said, I was here only to confirm what happened between you two, and I got my fucking answer. Now, if you'll excuse me, I need food," Steve let go of her restraint and marched away to get food while Sarah was left alone to think about what had happened.

She was infuriated, and her blood demanded revenge because getting banished meant they were alive. She wanted justice for her daughter, and in her head, she knew it was the only way she would be fine. She finally decided to move back to her quarters, letting it go for now.

As all three of them finally reached their quarters, Zachary closed the door behind them. Out of nowhere, Jason swung his fist in Xavier's face and kept punching him in a rage. Zachary ran towards the two and dragged him out of the quarrel.

"WHAT THE FUCK WERE YOU THINKING?" Jason screamed as he looked Xavier dead in the eye, but he stayed silent.

It was their first time seeing Xavier so devoid of emotions and speech. It was like they were talking to a walking corpse; all Xavier could do was stay silent. It was futile to reason with him in this state because Xavier was shunned by the entire moment. He opened up about a grueling memory he had wanted to forget for the longest time but never got the opportunity to.

"I'm sorry," Xavier mumbled under his breath, but it was not enough to satisfy Jason, who proceeded to leap forward again to punch him.

However, he was stopped by Zachary.

"STOP IT, JASON!" he screamed as he tossed him behind and aimed his battle knife on his face.

"Don't get any closer! I AM SICK AND TIRED OF EVERYTHING!" Zachary shouted, tearing up and gushing out tears. He did not want them to fight with one another since they were all that there was left of the group. In a sudden fit of despair, he started aiming the knife down his throat to take his own life but was quickly subdued by Xavier, who got stabbed in the palm instead.

"I don't want to live anymore. Just kill me. This is too much. I don't want this life anymore. I'm better off dead. We killed an innocent girl, Xavier! We killed a kid, and we tried to cover it up. What kind of monsters are we?!" Zachary cried out as Xavier held onto him.

Xavier started crying, too, and Jason just watched the two, letting out their emotions as they felt completely isolated from everything. At that moment, they felt so much pain and anxiety that they did not know what to do anymore. And just like that, the day passed, and nobody spoke to anyone afterward.

***

Jason woke up late at night, around 3 a.m., just to pack their stuff before leaving in the morning since they had been banished from the haven. There wasn't much they could do since Steve had not negotiated with them after that. Jason had gone and talked to him, trying his best to convince him to rethink his decision, but he was very adamant.

Jason sighed, lit a cigarette on the balcony, and just started smoking, thinking about what had happened that day and all the events that led them here, contemplating whether they were the good guys in this story and whether they had tried enough or not.

Just as he was immersed in his thoughts, he heard a loud noise from the kitchen, as if crockery had fallen from the racks. He slowly marched downstairs to investigate, and what he saw gave him the shock of his life. He ran instantly to find Xavier lying face-first on the floor.

"Xavier? Are you okay?" he asked, turning him over, his eyes widening at what he saw. He saw Xavier's neck split open as if someone had slit it with an axe or a sharp tool. He kept trying to wake him up, but one look into his lifeless eyes indicated that Xavier was dead.

Jason got up and started looking around, making his way to the kitchen to investigate the source of the loud sound, but he could not find anything. He slowly entered the lobby again and just held on to his fallen comrade, closing his eyes as he started to cry.

And with that, the night concluded with another grave loss.

Chapter 20: The Dead

There was no sun shining the next morning. Clouds covered the vast blue sky, making it evident that the black blanket was about to gush water onto the Earth. Sorrow filled the air, and everything felt sentimental. Zachary and Jason stood under the rain in the compound, along with Sarah, Steve, and his guards, who were deciding for them to leave.

Steve noticed something eerie; he saw Jason's face reddened with anger. He then looked at Zachary, whose face was tilted in utter disgust. He knew something had happened because Xavier was missing. He then looked at Sarah, who did not make eye contact at all. However, he stayed silent and drank his beer as he smirked, watching the silence stretch among them.

"Oi, where's the other wanker?" Steve asked Jason with a smirk, but he got no answer.

He then looked at Zachary and asked the same question again, but he, too, remained silent. The silence annoyed Steve so much that he flung his hand in the air, snapped two of his fingers, and gestured to the guards to bring in something.

"I have a surprise fo' ya dilly dalliers. Hope you love it!" he shouted, chuckling loudly as the guards brought in a body bag.

The guards tossed it right at Jason's feet, and one of them instantly opened it. It revealed the corpse of Xavier, his neck now decayed, flies buzzing around the open wound. Maggots were devouring his eyes.

Zachary vomited as soon as he saw the rotting body and coughed out his lungs while the guards quickly covered up the dead man.

"So, which one of y'all is responsible for this rut?" Steve asked, sitting down on one of his chairs.

"I mean, I give it to you; you lads are bonkers enough to feed a child to those wankers," he scoffed and downed his beer, tossing it at the body bag.

This infuriated Jason, who charged at him but was instantly dragged out of the scene by the guards.

"I'LL FUCKING KILL YOU!" Jason shouted just as he was hit in the shoulder by a baton.

"Easy there, twat! I didn't do this fuckery," Steve responded nonchalantly.

He approached Jason, who was now pinned against the ground. He unholstered his revolver and tapped it on Jason's skull multiple times, the smirk never leaving his face.

"So, which one of you was throwing a wobbly? Eh?"

Steve got up and looked around, trying to meet everyone's eyes. He saw as everyone looked at him, but Sarah hid them completely.

"Alrighty, let's play a game, shall we? I will spin this revolver, and whoever this twat lands on speaks. And if they don't, my revolver will do the speaking for them."

He loosened the gun on his finger and spun it multiple times. Everyone looked on in horror as the revolver spun on his finger; they knew his ferocity. After a few seconds, the gun stopped, pointing toward one of the guards.

"You, wanker, talk." He aimed it right at his face.

"I- I don't know what hap-"

Before he could even finish his sentence, Steve had shot his brains out. Everyone stared as the smirk on Steve's face turned into a death stare.

"How the fuck are you motherfucker's guards if you don't even know what you're guarding?"

He marched toward the dead guard and spat at his corpse, kicking off the dirt from his shoes as he looked back at the crowd. He spun his gun on his fingers again, marching toward all of them slowly. Everyone slowly backed up as they saw Steve's eyes shoot open, glaring everyone down. At that moment, Jason realized who they were messing with; in his eyes, Steve was no more than the Grim Reaper.

The gun stopped at Zachary now, and Jason's heart instantly dropped as he started crawling desperately towards him.

"No, Steve, stop, please!" Jason screamed as he clawed on the floor but was dragged away by the guards.

"You, talk."

Steve spoke as he removed the safety once again and pulled his finger to the trigger at the miserable Zachary. The shock of seeing his friend dead and almost decayed had rendered him unable to speak, and within a second, Steve pulled the trigger.

Panic ensued everywhere, but silence followed right after. Even the sound of birds chirping was not heard, nor were the soft sounds of the downpour. The only thing that was heard was Zachary's heavy breathing; he hadn't been shot. Instead, it was one of the guards who had been shot down, falling right in front of Zachary. He hadn't shouted or screamed since it had all happened so suddenly.

Sarah immediately gripped Steve's collar, infuriated at this random killing spree. But he was unfazed and proceeded to reload his revolver.

"What the fuck is wrong with you?!" she shouted. "You're supposed to dispose of them quickly!"

"Don't be so serious. I was only taking the piss," Steve scoffed, shrugging and rubbing the tip of the revolver on his head in agitation.

"Why are you dropping down our men, one by one? Is this necessary?" Sarah snapped back at his attitude.

"I mean, isn't that what you did?" Steve tilted his head and raised an eyebrow, smirking at her.

Sarah was left shaken; she began questioning whether it was all a bluff or if it really was the truth spoken from his mouth. Regardless, she stayed silent and glared him down.

"Were you chuffed when he was wilting in pain, laddie?" he added as he aimed the revolver right at Sarah's head.

As soon as he did, she began shaking.

"You think I'm stupid? Eh? This town ain't big enough to muffle out all that ruckus now, is it?" Steve continued.

All this talking had shocked Jason. He had honestly thought that Xavier was killed by one of Steve's men as an act of revenge for Sarah. But it turned out this wasn't the case. Sarah had acted out on her own. It still didn't change that both knew each other, so it felt like a collective effort had contributed to Xavier's demise. Jason thought it seemed like a scripted conversation so Sarah could spy on them.

"Jason, Zachary, and you, all three, get the fuck out of my town," Steve responded, beginning to walk away from them.

"Y-You can't do this to me, Steve," Sarah quivered as she spoke, but Steve just kept walking off.

"I'm absolutely knackered! I need a bevvy," Steve shouted as the rest of the guards followed him.

A few guards immediately ran to the compound and dragged out two of the corpses, and the rest escorted all three of them to the gate, leaving them with no supplies. So now, the two and the person who had killed their friend were en route into the unknown with no hopes of survival.

***

The guards carried the dead bodies to the beverage room, back in the Haven. They tossed the bodies on the floor, and they all felt utterly disgusted as they stood in front of a door leading to a secret room.

The room was full of the grueling scent of blood and rotting flesh; it felt like someone had died there ages ago, and it had never been cleaned. The room had one bulb hanging on the ceiling, which was the only source of light, and the only thing visible was a dark silhouette growling in the distance.

The guards slowly walked in halfway and tossed the bodies into the room, slowly making their way to the exit as they did not want to make any noise. But they stopped as Steve showed up and closed the door behind the guards.

Both instantly ran towards the door and started banging on it, trying their best to escape. They forgot they were not alone in that room as panic engulfed them from head to toe.

"Sir, let us out!" shouted one of the guards, who began panicking.

"Boss, please! Spare us! We didn't do anything!" screamed the other.

"That's exactly why I shouldn't spare you. We had a traitor amongst us, and none of you wankers did anything about it," Steve answered as he walked away from the room, closing the door and dropping the blinds.

They both began screaming and crying in pain, being ripped to shreds by whatever demon Steve kept on the inside.

The other guards who had come in to assist Steve lowered their gaze as they saw Steve approaching them. But he walked past them, drinking his booze while the guards inside shouted their throats raw, wanting to get out of the horrors of that room, but within mere seconds, all that screaming had converted into silence.

***

“Ah great, we’re walking with the fucking enemy,” Zachary spoke as he kicked the nearby bush.

“Enemy?! You bastards killed my da-”

Before Sarah could complete her sentence, Jason interrupted her.

“Madam, with all due respect, if your daughter was bit, she was already dead.”

“SHE WAS NO-”

Jason interrupted her again.

“Screaming it out loud will not change that fact more than the fact that she is also dead. Move the fuck on. Quite literally, too.”

“You would never understand,” she mouthed, spitting at Jason.

He, however, did not react.

“All right, all those in favor of feeding the crazy lady to the fucking zombies?” Jason asked, raising his hand immediately after that without hesitation.

Zachary joined him in this as well. But as soon as they were about to say anything, she drew the knife she hid in her belt and pointed it right at them.

“I’ll fucking kill all of you. EVERY SINGLE ONE OF YOU!”

She began charging at Jason, but he easily disarmed her and held her in a headlock.

"Go to sleep, PLEASE!" he yelled, hitting her cranium with the back of the blade, rendering her unconscious.

He sighed as soon as she fell on the floor, and since he couldn't leave her alone defenseless, he had to carry her on his back.

"What are you doing?" Zachary asked as he looked at him.

"We have to do something about it now, don't we?" Jason answered as he started walking towards the wood.

"She's not our responsibility, Jason. She killed Xavier," He spoke, following him.

"Yeah, but we can't just leave her there?!" Jason snapped at him, looking back.

"Look, you might have lost your shit, but I didn't, alright? I still wanna survive this shit. I don't want to die," he added to the conversation.

"I get tha-"

Zachary was interrupted by Jason again.

"NO! It's you FUCKERS who don't understand that I had to carry all your shits with me! I had to handle you two, I had to take care of you two, I had to make sure both of you were all right. I AM TIRED! Spare me, for fuck's sake! Let me do whatever the fuck I want to now because I'm tired of doing everything everyone wants me to," he added, his eyes heavy from all the tears he held to himself.

All the times he had held his composure were taking a toll on him all at once now.

So, Zachary followed him as he began marching into the forest they had just come out of. He made sure he was close to him so that he could keep tabs on him. As they kept walking, time slowly passed, and it was already getting dark since they had been walking all morning and afternoon. Jason was convinced they were lost, but Zachary insisted on staying on foot because stopping somewhere was risky. They eventually led themselves to a nearby lake, which was vast enough to make camp. So, they eventually set up their tents there.

The sun showed its sparkle for a moment, but it eventually faded into the sky as the dusk finally rose, and so did the dangers of being stranded in a secluded forest full of nothing but darkness.

Jason started a fire by the lake and set up tents for all three of them. In one of the tents, he placed all his belongings and checked if his gun had any more bullets to spare, but unfortunately, he had three rounds left in it. Zachary had no weapons on him because he had dropped all of them beforehand, so he was only left with Jason's battle knife.

In the meantime, Sarah woke up and made her way outside, seeing Jason and Zachary by the fire, making fried fish they had caught from the lake.

She sighed and sat down with them. Jason offered her a serving of the fish, which she ate slowly, her head still hurt from the strike Jason had made on her skull.

"Take it easy. That hit could've given you a concussion if I was too clumsy," Jason spoke as he ate the fish.

"Thanks for nothing, I guess," she mouthed as she began eating.

"Thanks for keeping it quiet," Jason scoffed as he offered his fish to Zachary.

"Thank you," Zachary whispered as he began to eat.

"Now, we need to be careful. We don't know what's lurking in this forest. We need to be on guard, but one of us can't do it all alone, so we will take turns, mhm?" Jason spoke as he held onto his gun and got up.

"I don't agree with that," Sarah responded.

"You're on your own. If one lurker shows up and they're devouring you, don't expect any of us to come and save you."

Jason's reply was cold and stern, as he did not hesitate before answering and made his way into the vast distance.

"Also, if I'm not here in 10 minutes, run," he added, leaving with a flashlight and loading his gun with all three rounds he had.

Zachary and Sarah were left on the logs, sitting and eating slowly. Zachary felt uncomfortable since he was sitting with his comrade's killer, but there was nothing much he could do about it. She saw as cold sweats began emitting from his forehead, taking that moment to speak to him.

"You were there when it happened, weren't you?"

Silence maintained itself as Zachary did not respond and continued eating his fish.

"I asked you something," Sarah spoke, her tone rising.

"Can we please move on?" Zachary inquired, looking at her with absolutely no emotions on his face.

It ticked Sarah off, and she got up and approached him with the sharp stick she had in her grasp.

"You both took everything from me, and I'll do the exact same thing," she smirked as she approached him but was stopped in her way.

A gun was pointed right at the back of her head; it was Jason who had approached them sneakily because he still did not trust Sarah enough to leave his comrade with her.

"Take one more step. I'll reunite you with your daughter."

Jason spoke without hesitation, shocking Zachary as he had never seen him this cold.

Jason placed his finger on the trigger, ready to shoot, but Sarah backed off.

"Get going. It's your turn," he spoke, aiming the gun right at her.

"I won't go," she snapped back.

"We're leaving, Zachary. If she follows you in any way, kill her on sight," he said as Zachary nodded.

After a few minutes of silence, Sarah decided to comply with the lot and left without a word. She was given her weapon so she could defend herself, but she couldn't be given anything lethal since Jason knew she was unstable.

She walked into the woods, and Jason sighed and sat beside Zachary.

"Man, why do we always get stuck with assholes, terminators, and fucking unstable people?" he asked.

"Bad luck, I guess?" Zachary chuckled nervously, beginning to eat Jason's fish as well.

“Hey! That’s mine!” he shouted as he grabbed onto the stick, and they both began play-fighting.

“Jason, I’m very hungry! C’mon!” Zachary spoke as he kept pulling the stick.

“Man, I’ve been taking care of you guys. I need my energy!” he screamed as he pulled the stick and munched on the fish instantly.

Zachary’s face dropped in sorrow, as he was very hungry. But since Jason was considerate enough to care for everyone, he shared some of his fish with him.

“Eat up, you big baby,” Jason spoke as he chuckled.

They both had a slight moment of relaxation, but it was short-lived as they immediately heard a loud screech. They both got up and immediately followed the noise, calling out Sarah, but she did not respond.

“I swear if I see another fucked up zombie, I’m going to lose my mind,” Jason spoke as they were running into the woods.

He reloaded his gun and gave his knife to Zachary. They both made it to the site where the noise had emitted from, and as soon as they reached there, their hearts dropped beating. What they saw scared the living hell out of them.

"It had to be a fucked-up zombie. It just had to be one," Jason mouthed as his eyes dimmed out from the panic he felt inside his chest.

They saw an abomination: a six-foot-tall creature, its mouthpiece missing the lower jaw, hair growing out on its body, and its eyes glowing piercing red. It snarled menacingly towards them as it had a part of a human intestine stuck to one of its teeth. Its legs were covered entirely in decaying wounds, and its chest was completely open, exposing its flesh from the inside out. Hair covered its face, which only made the glowing red eyes visible, but before any of them could do anything about it, it fled immediately from contact.

"So, is nobody going to point out the fact that we just saw a fucking werewolf?" Jason looked at Zachary, who marched away to check up on Sarah, who was found lying on the floor, too shunned even to speak.

"Are you okay? Did it bite you?" Zachary asked as he began examining her exposed limbs, upon which he found a big scratch on her leg.

"No, I tripped on a tree branch," she said, pointing at the nearby branch.

"Are you fucking sure?" Jason marched in and checked for the wound, but she immediately hid it with a cloth since it was bleeding way too much.

"Yeah, I'm fine. Let's get out of here," Sarah answered as she got up.

"Hold the fuck up, we're not going anywhere, what happened?" Jason interrogated further as he aimed the gun at her.

"You really wanna do this here and get eaten by whatever that was?" Sarah asked him in a state of panic.

"I don't care if an elephant's corpse walks in on me anymore. I've seen enough! You answer my fucking question!" Jason snapped back as he aimed the gun at her head.

"I swear, I swear I wasn't bit, I swear!"

She started crying and screaming, and Zachary grabbed onto Jason's shoulder, saying,

"Let's do this somewhere else, man. We can't have more sound, you know what we saw."

After a brief battle within himself, Jason lowered the gun and began walking towards the campsite but stayed on his guard as they both walked. However, he made sure Sarah walked in front of them so that they could examine her. As she stepped forward, Jason noticed how she began limping after walking normally, felt cold, and immediately dropped to one knee after a while. Zachary had to carry her back to the tents and lay her down later, as they both witnessed it all happening to her.

Zachary looked at Jason and immediately gave him that look he gave when they had to deal with Morgan, but they both let it slide and decided to stay up all night and guard the situation as much as they could. Unbeknownst to them, that night would eventually change everything.

***

Jason woke up suddenly at night as he had passed out from fatigue that had appeared out of nowhere. He stretched and saw that Zachary was nowhere to be found. It stressed him out because Zachary never left alone and informed him every single time. Regardless, he got up and slowly made his way toward the tent, only for his legs to stop immediately.

He didn't know why he stopped there, but his body awaited his response. He slowly tilted his head to his side, and as soon as it was stuck in place, the sight horrified him; Sarah was feasting on Zachary's neck, ripping it apart piece by piece as his corpse lay there experiencing it all.

Sarah slowly turned her neck and began growling at Jason, who shot her immediately in the face. It blasted open her jaw, but she didn't fall. She started crawling towards him, and she got faster with every step she took. Fearing he'd run out of bullets before he shot down the lurker, he began to run, and Sarah followed close behind.

Now, she didn't run and leap like a normal zombie; instead, she was jumping on the trees to follow him.

"I swear to fucking God," Jason cursed and shook his head as he began running with all his strength.

But it wasn't long before Sarah got closed in on him, growling like an animal, and finally leaped towards him and bit onto his neck.

"FUCK!" Jason screamed in pain as she began biting down with all her might, but Jason finally managed to get her off him, wasting all his lead and delivering the final blow.

He had used up all the ammo in his gun, and the gunshots caused him to go deaf in his left ear since it had been too close to his face. But the shots sent Sarah flying into a nearby tree. Her brain splattered on the tree bark, and her groaning immediately stopped, finally being put out of her misery.

Jason was now left with a flesh wound from a zombie, struggling to deal with the fact that he was going to become the living dead. So, with a great sigh, he started walking towards the safest place he could lie down and decay into absolutely nothing since he was out of bullets and weapons. He walked, and with every step he took, his vision slowly became blurry, his throat got dry, his eyes began to bleed, and his wound began to reek. He was finally experiencing everything Morgan had to deal with, and his heart started pumping fast, feeling the hunger consume him. After walking for 20 minutes, he fell right next to a tree, groaning and sighing as his body finally gave off strength.

Within that moment, someone approached him slowly as they unholstered a familiar revolver. He thought it was Zachary because that was the only word Jason could utter; his friend's gruesome death really depressed him, and the guilt of not being able to save him ate him more than the virus. The man casually sat down and aimed the revolver right down Jason's mouth, aiming on top as he scoffed.

"How do ya like my new toy?"

It was Steve.

"Ya' saw the werewolf wanker, din't ya?" he further inquired as he pulled the trigger before Jason could even utter a word, shooting out his brains in an instant.

"No hard feelings, Jason. My toy was knackered," Steve spoke as he got up, wiping the blood off his face with a napkin and tossing it right back at the dead corpse.

"Clean yourself up when this shit is done, 'kay?" Steve added as he strolled off into the woods in silence.

The silence stretched long as Jason's dead corpse lay dormant there before it was welcomed by red gleaming eyes closing in on the dead man. The silence was interrupted by a growling that was beginning to rumble louder and louder now, ensuring Jason Foster's demise.

Made in the USA
Columbia, SC
27 April 2024

d338f22c-dfc9-4c44-a4a8-e39efaaafd1aR02